Theory of the Case

A Novel
by

TR Pearson

Barking Mad Press

CHUCKATUCK

TR Pearson

i

"Hey, listen."

I'd decided that was probably all he could say. It was the only thing I'd ever heard out of him all the times that I'd walked past him, and he was in a place where people babbled, sat in silence, or did worse, so it seemed like that was what he had instead of conversation.

Somebody kept him nice. His clothes were always buttoned and zipped and tidy, but I can't say I ever saw any family. It would be just him sitting out in the hall. The ladies there tried to move him around and get him involved with all the stuff the other residents got up to, but he'd ease back down with his walker and park again in his usual spot.

His room was somewhere else entirely. The hall where he sat went nowhere much. It started at a drink box and ended at a fire door with three closets and two toilets in between. There were five chairs on a frame like you'd find in an airport terminal. He liked the one in the middle, and I'd often see him when I'd go for a soda or a pee.

"Hey, listen."

I was out there watching my uncle die. Homer
was the youngest, the last of my mother's clan.
He wasn't sick exactly, just old and tired and
failing, and he'd gotten to where he slept most all
the time. Homer would wake up long enough to
sip some juice and wonder who you were. Then
he'd grumble and burp and sink directly back
under.

I never knew him all that well those years he
was awake. He'd lived in Idaho or somewhere.
Homer had worked as a builder and then had
gone into ranching. The story was he took a herd
of cows in lieu of pay for a barn roof. It seems
Homer was paranoid and crotchety by the time he
made forty-five and hardly worth talking to once
he'd hit sixty. He found a woman somehow and
followed her east. They lived a few years in
Newport News. Then she jilted him or passed
away, and Uncle Homer started dozing.

I'd made a promise to my mother that I'd keep
tabs on the guy, or I wouldn't have troubled
myself to swing by once a week to see him. It's
hard to know what good you do by watching blood
kin sleep. I'd bring books and mean to read them,
but it was a chore to sit in his room. Homer
snored mightily and smelled like a stockyard, so I
did more than a little wandering, decided my
mother wouldn't have cared.

Homer had ended up in the usual, sprawling geriatric warehouse. Magnolia Hills was what they called it. No magnolias. No hills either. Just a Bojangles half a mile up the road and a muddy finger of the James River down the other way. The place was not at all convenient to the interstate, and the closest town of any size was an unincorporated speed trap with two churches, a car wash, and a diner that closed at two in the afternoon.

I only had kind of a job at the time. I'd been effectively retired when I took work from a neighbor who'd promised not to need me much. I drove him when his regular guy had a day off or a court date. He used a Chrysler New Yorker for an office and had me carry him around the greater Norfolk area. Benny gave himself out as a freelance entrepreneur, but he was effectively a loan shark with a taste for Handel operas and a sadistic streak.

Benny had cerebral palsy and got around with a dogwood staff. He spoke pretty well but was fairly moist at it and probably seemed weak and compromised until he throttled you once.

His conscience — to the extent he had one — was always retroactive. "Why did you go and make me do that?" was how it usually showed itself. Rare was the man with the nerve or teeth to answer Benny back.

As long as he was armed with his dogwood staff, Benny had no need for muscle, so I just drove where he told me, changed his cd's when he asked, and mashed up his food for lunch so he could swallow it without choking.

For his part, Benny made phone calls and paid visits to delinquent clients. That's what he always called them, even the ones he battered and beat. Benny was proper and courtly in his fashion, particular about the tone of things. He always paid me more than I'd earned and thanked me without fail for my time and indulgence, which I'd decided was compensation enough for a potential accessory beef.

I often worked two, occasionally three days a week, which left me plenty of time to honor the pledge I'd made to my mother. On Thursdays usually I'd drive to Magnolia Hills and watch Uncle Homer sleep. I did a fair bit of wandering the hallways — dementia, bridge, TV, the odd dandruffy preacher, the sweet scorched stink of Nescafe.

"Hey, listen."

He told me at first his name was Walt, and then he decided it was Dan, and I doubt I would have taken the time to sit and hear him out if Homer hadn't gone incontinent and needed to get cleaned off. A couple of ladies were swabbing him tip to toe one Thursday when I arrived, so I went on a wander and ended up at the drink box. Walt/ Dan was in his usual spot. I left a chair between us and sat.

"Hey, listen."

I had a slug of Sundrop and told the man, "All right."

I was accustomed to the residents in that place saying crazy things my way, usually about the staff being up to some kind of treachery. Spiking the food. Stealing the drugs. Shifting the furniture at night. I expected something similar from Walt/Dan in the hallway.

"Abigail Tucker. No middle name. You can look her up."

I waited for more, but he seemed to be finished. "Why?" I asked him. "Who's she?"

But I didn't exist for Walt/Dan any longer. He'd found the red fire alarm across the hall and was looking at that instead.

I stayed long enough to finish my soda and then headed back to Homer. He was snoring and smelling like a blend of Pine Sol and raccoon.

I didn't think about Abigail Tucker again for nearly two solid weeks, not until I got reminded of her by a business call of Benny's. He'd had me swing by a coffee bar between Suffolk and the beltway, a cute little place in a spot where six or eight businesses had died. You had to turn against traffic to reach it, and then you couldn't get back out — a problem the owners discovered after they'd spent a fair bit of Benny's money on a pricey four-gang espresso machine and Etruscan tile for the floor.

It was dogwood staff day for those coffee people, their inaugural taste of bad Benny, and once he went in and laid out a barista, all the rest of them came rushing out. They had uniforms, long black aprons, wore bow ties and paper hats, like soda jerks on prom night. Their glossy name tags were ceramic. The two guys who owned the place were plainly detail oriented and had gotten everything but the commerce part of it right.

Benny was conveying as much inside while the hourly wagers fretted in the lot. One of them wept loudly into the hem of her apron. I got a look at her ceramic tag. Abigail was her name.

"Oh, right," I told myself. "Abigail Tucker," and pulled out my phone.

There proved to be scores of Abigail Tuckers. One was a doctor with a radio show. One was a minister in Atlanta. One was an internet sensation with no modesty and a tan. I got sidetracked by photos she'd posted due to her quasi-hypnotic cleavage, but then I had to give her up for a bit while I answered questions from baristas.

"He going to kill them?" was, in essence, the thing they most wanted to know.

We were hearing the occasional shout and anguished cry from inside the shop. Crockery breaking too. Benny was big on busting stuff for effect. He didn't care if that made it harder for people who owed him cash to pay.

"Can't seem all there," he explained to me once. "They won't get the right kind of scared."

So it sure sounded like homicide in the offing, but I tried to calm the employees.

"Mostly a banking issue," I told them. Then glass broke and a grown man screamed.

Out of all the Abigail Tuckers, only one was something like local, and the best I could tell, she'd been dead for fourteen years. I couldn't get at the article about her because I didn't have an active account with the Times-Dispatch, so I dropped her for another couple of weeks until I was sitting on my front stoop one evening and my neighbor's boy came over to give me money for beer.

They'd named him Dwight — not after the supreme allied commander but some country singer his mother had a thing for in the day.

Dwight was fifteen and round. Nearsighted. Asthmatic. I bought Dwight Red Stripe in exchange for computer stuff. I could barely work my phone, and he was a digital-age savant.

Dwight mostly did his computer magic for girls he knew from school. He'd change their grades, buy them clothes with plundered credit cards, rewrite their enemies' facebook posts, deblotch their selfies. They'd pay him often with the sort of sex that only seems to count for boys.

"Abigail Tucker," I told him. "I'm figuring Virginia girl. Find her for me?"

Dwight nodded. I went and fetched the twelve pack I'd carried home for him and left the business in his hands. It was a week, maybe ten days later when he came back over with his laptop. Dwight only ever got around to my stuff once he'd run low on beer.

"Probably this one or this one," he said and showed me two girls on his screen. One girl anyway and one full-blown woman whose credit union colleagues had thrown her a party and posted pictures of it online.

"Was this one in the Richmond paper?" I pointed at the girl.

Dwight nodded and pulled up the article. Sixteen. Strawberry blonde. Gummy smile.

"What does it say?"

"Dead," Dwight told me. "Went missing in 2002. Hunter found her body, 2004."

"Murdered?"

Dwight nodded.

"Who by?"

"Doesn't say." He scrolled. He read. "Found her in Simmons Gap."

"Where's that?"

Dwight mapped it for me and showed me his laptop screen. Simmons Gap looked to be in a crease of terrain on the eastern edge of Shenandoah National Park.

"She from out there?"

Dwight did more scanning and scrolling. "Chuckatuck. Ran away or something." He shifted his screen to show me a headstone in what looked like a pasture.

I knew Chuckatuck. Benny had a couple of hardheads there. One who broke bones for him when Benny was swamped and needed a proxy and one who owned a garage and was always trying to pay Benny back in tires. Chuckatuck's one of those glad-I'm-not-from-here places that you ride through and tell yourself, "Nope." I decided Hey, listen was probably the dead girl's father or uncle or something and his arteries had hardened just enough to put her on his brain, and then I went a couple of months and didn't think any more about it.

Homer got truly sick. It was October by then. I'd known something was up with him because he was gurgling when he snored, and it turned into pneumonia outright in between my Thursday visits. One week I left him asleep and gurgling. The next week I found him in a tent.

An actual nurse was at the bedside checking the oxygen flow to Homer.

"Had a bit of a crisis," she told me and then said lots of medical stuff.

Homer, for his part, was sleeping. I could see him through the plastic.

"He going to make it?"

That earned me an arm pat. A tight smile. "We'll see".

Enough raw oxygen had found its way into the room to make my throat scratchy and sore, so I 'visited' Homer by taking a walking tour of Magnolia Hills. Outside first. The grounds were lovely and well-tended, but some brainiac landscape architect had designed them to be bumpy like the property had broken out in boils. It was no good for wheelchairs and rolling walkers, so the residents stayed hard by the building where the terrain was flat.

I got winded doing a circuit at my regular trudge and rewarded myself with a soda and a sit.

"Hey, listen."

"Oh, right. Chuckatuck," I told Walt/Dan.

That gave him a jolt and some focus. He shifted around to look at me. He was all nose hair and milky eyes.

"She your daughter?"

"Eight seven three nine four six stroke B."

Not enough digits for a phone or a social. "What's that?" He looked to be sinking or wavering or something. "Simmons Gap, right?"

He sucked air like he'd surfaced from a quarter mile down and then made a pitiful whimper of a noise and nodded.

"Who's she to you?"

You never know what'll wake them up once they've reached the sleepy stages, that part of life where you can pass a day just sitting in a hall. A lot of times nothing will. That was Homer through and through, but Walt/Dan had a button, and I'd found it.

He leaned my way, so I leaned his. He told me, "Everything."

They sent one of the ladies for me, Denise. She was large and brown and jolly and always ready with a smile and wink. "He woke up in a bad way," she said and asked me to come with her. I

assumed Homer was fading and in terminal
trouble, but it turned out the pure oxygen had
revived him a little too well. I found him
explaining eugenics to a Nigerian orderly named
Kim, a large, powerful blue-black gentleman
possessed of the grace to let Homer live.

Just Homer's head was sticking out of his tent.
He immediately quit on the master race once I'd
come into the room and started in about his sister
who'd married Maryland trash. "And look what it
got," he said of me.

I sort of hated the thought of a Homer back to
what passed with him for normal. Luckily, he just
coughed a few times and then drew back into his
tent and went to sleep.

"That man in the hall . . . "

"Mr. Demarest," Denise told me.

"Did he used to be a cop?"

"Don't think so." She looked towards the
orderly. "Didn't he own a store or something?"

The big blue-black Nigerian nodded. "Sunoco.
Chuckatuck," he said.

~~~

I have a friend. She has a husband, but neither
one of us likes him much. I met her in Trader
Joe's over a sack of frozen dumplings. I was
trying to grab a bag, but she was blocking the case

with her cart, so I was having to do some ambitious leaning in when I noticed she was crying. That doesn't quite cover it actually. She was sobbing on the shumai.

I did that smooth thing guys are known for, asked her, "Lady, are you all right?"

She wept harder, louder. I was starting to get a weird kind of attention in the aisle. Then she grabbed her own sack of dumplings and flung it into her cart before she grabbed my shirt sleeve and thoroughly swabbed her face.

Her car, a Volvo wagon, was parked beside the cart chute with all of the windows down. I heard her before I saw her. She'd crawled into the back seat and was having another heaving warble. I looked around the lot for a mental health professional, but it was just me, a couple of Mexican roofers, and an airedale in a Saab.

"Want me to call somebody?" I asked her.

She told her leather upholstery, "No." Then she shifted to have a look at me. "Oh. You," she said.

I showed her my palms — the universal symbol for I'm-walking-the-hell-away-from-your-mess-right-now, and I was very nearly safe and clear when she spoke up and told me, "Hey."

"What?"

"Come here."

I thought about not going back but pictured her flinging herself into traffic. She was just as I'd left her, stretched out on her back. She gave me a thorough once over, wiped her nose with a knuckle.

When she didn't speak, I chimed in. "Want me to buy you a coffee or something?"

I'm pretty sure we've never had coffee, and we've spent untold hours together. I'm still not entirely clear on her name, but I get by calling her Gus. When she calls me anything it's 'you' or 'buddy', but we're not too big on talking.

That first afternoon we ended up having sex in my coat closet. I'd call it love making if that even remotely captured what it was. We didn't need to be in the coat closet since we were the only ones at home, but she found the closet rod stout enough to let her do what she needed, which were pull ups primarily that I stood by and helped her make worthwhile.

We didn't talk after or share a cigarette or marvel at the depth of our connection. Instead she wandered through my house and sneered at all my possessions, drew a half a glass of tap water and drank it. I think she told me, "So," before she let herself out the back door.

It seems now that many weeks went by before I strayed across her again. I was trying to find an arcane piece of plumbing that had failed in my half bath, some kind of brass valve that nobody had manufactured for ages. The way plumbing jobs invariably work for me is I try to make a repair and either I can't get the part or I break something else in the process of putting it in. Then I escalate to fixtures and haul home a couple of those before it's midnight and I'm obliged to cut off the water at the main. The following morning I call a proper plumber, and he renovates the bathroom.

So I was early on in the process — had a drip I couldn't live with — when I was standing in front of assorted valves at a Home Depot in outer Norfolk. A kid came by. I'm not good with kid's ages. He's was about four feet tall, and the aisle was clotted with people and pipes, so he was having trouble slipping through on his scooter. It was one of those shiny folding things that should have been left in the car.

For whatever reason, he picked me out as the fleshbag he'd engage with and ran straight into me, clipped my ankle.

"Get out of the way," he said.

In the ordinary course of things, I don't care terribly much for children, most especially this modern crop. I dumped the kid off his scooter and tossed it onto a shelf overhead where it clattered around and disappeared between two water heaters. Then I went back to failing to find the right valve while the kid screamed at me and whined.

His dad showed up. He was just like his son only nearly six feet and doughy. "What the hell's this?"

Once his boy had explained it all to him, dad came closing on me hard.

For most men fighting is like full-contact ballroom dancing. A couple of guys get aggravated or offended. They bark back and forth, make threats. They've seen real punches thrown on TV and decide to give it a try, but they lack the timing and balance so, usually, glorified wrestling ensues.

I can't say I was ever a beast, but I'd long worked in a world where you needed to know how to catch a guy flush on the windpipe or step into a straight left with all your weight behind it, and there was comfort in the knowledge that most men are pretty much like scooter boy's dad.

He made fists, like they do, closed snug and gave me the eyeball.

"Your kid's a jerk," I told him. "Best fix it while you can."

That failed to have a calming effect. He shoved me, so I hit him, gave him a short, crisp shot to the throat, and he started wheezing and weaving and feeling around. I grabbed his collar and lowered him so he could sit without banging his head.

"Scooter's up with the water heaters," I told him.

The kid wailed at me further as I went back to not finding the valve I needed, and then I heard a voice I recognized. "Jeremy?" she said.

Gus came along and stopped at her husband's side. He was sitting on the floor for some reason. "What are you doing?"

Gus and I shared a glance as her miserable kid gave her the blow by blow. Then I left for the next aisle over to find the fixture I'd fail to connect.

She stopped by that very evening and scratched on my back screen door like a cat. I was mopping up water in the bathroom where the shower rod wouldn't support her. I didn't feel much like the coat closet, so we ended up in bed —near it anyway — and afterwards we had something approaching a conversation.

"He makes good money," she told me.

"Hope so," was all I said.

ii

Benny's regular driver has a road rage problem. It's not job-related aggression but recreational assaults, and Marco can't seem to avoid them. I know Benny has talked to him about it, and he even sent Marco on a course — six sessions with a half dozen of the similarly afflicted up at a Richmond church, but a scant week later Marco got behind an erratic Chinese driver who signaled and then failed to turn for longer than Marco could endure.

Worse still, the man spoke broken English, so Marco felt he had to slug him since Marco's a chauvinistic American patriot even if Dominican by birth. Benny decided not to make the usual payments to the usual court officials, so Marco ended up doing ninety days, which meant I worked steady for a stretch. I kept Thursdays aside for Homer, but it was the Chrysler the rest of the week.

I came during that time to fuller understanding of Benny's territory and scope. He had reach and suasion from the Dismal Swamp west all the way to Emporia and north as far as Jamestown, maybe Charles City in a pinch. On my part-time days we rarely strayed terribly far from Norfolk, but once I was doing solid weeks, we covered most everything from Richmond east.

Benny had a thing about Virginia Beach and refused to do business there. I found out in time there'd been a woman. She was born around Fort Story, and she'd played on Benny's affections and had scammed him in the end. Since she wasn't around to get detested in the flesh, Benny hated her birthplace instead.

"Where'd she go?" I remember asking Marco.

"Don't know." Then he explained that the gulf stream could take a lady most anywhere.

That was the thing I always tried to remember about Benny. A man's whose conscience is retroactive doesn't, in truth, much have one at all. Benny never thought in terms of morals or doing what was right. He was all about levels of exposure he could tolerate and satisfaction he could possibly extract. Otherwise, he had a taste for Handel operas and a mild case of CP. There wasn't a lot to Benny like there's not much to a cobra.

I met him because he fell down. Benny slipped on wet grass in his yard, and I was out trying to help Dwight and his mother find Percy, their calico cat. Percy had knocked out a window screen and gone for a wander, so we were walking up and down the block calling for him as if a cat might possibly come.

Benny was watering his decorative grasses and had laid his dogwood stick aside. His place was nothing fancy at all, just a faux Tudor eyesore with azaleas up against the foundation and decorative plantings here and there. I'd seen Benny around and had been warned off of him by both Dwight and his mother, so I knew he was halt and shaky and more than a little malicious, but when I came across him sprawled in his yard, I couldn't just leave him there.

I stuck out my hand. He took it, and I hoisted him to his feet. I didn't ask him if he was all right. He didn't trouble himself to thank me, and I went back out into the road to look for that stinking cat.

It turned out that was all Benny needed to persuade him I was made of stuff he liked. Since then, I've seen him arrive at all sorts of judgments about people based on hardly anything. He's no better at it than most but has decided that he is.

Right at the start of my three-month stint driving Benny steady, we ended up in Chuckatuck one afternoon for lunch. Benny had made a couple of painless collections down around King's Fork, and he was pleased with the orchestration and pace of a new Rodelinda CD. It featured Anne Sofie von Otter, who Benny had a thing for,

and the picture of her on the front of the box sure
made her look like a willowy dish.

So it was shaping up to be a fine and stirring
day for Benny, and he had me pull in at a Subway
and buy us each a tuna salad. Benny had been
avoiding the stuff because he was vain and feared
he was getting a gut.

I didn't realize we were in Chuckatuck until I'd
already mashed up his sandwich. Benny over
manufactured drool, luxuriated in it, and he had
to work to keep it seeping from his mouth
whenever he ate. We sat at a table out back by the
propane tank where I tied on Benny's towel and
left him to shove his pulverized sandwich in
however he saw fit. It wasn't an activity you
wanted to watch up close, especially when
mayonnaise was involved, so I stayed by in case
he needed me but made out to be captivated by a
sign — a big billboard just up the blacktop for the
Chuckatuck Garden Center.

"You remember," I asked Benny, "a Sunoco
around here?"

He rapped on the table and pointed at the
ground.

"This was it?"

Benny gagged and gurgled. He was kind of a
spectacle when stuff went in his mouth, which is
why he ate at picnic tables alongside propane

tanks or leaning against the passenger door in the back seat of his New Yorker. Benny had a fear of seeming vulnerable and weak, which made sense given the business he was in, given the sort of people he dealt with.

"Green one?" I asked. He nodded. And I got up and went round to get Benny his usual luncheon Gatorade.

The place was now an up-to-date grocery mart/ Subway/gas station. I had to think they'd probably leveled Walt/Dan's Sunoco, just cleared the lot and started fresh, so I wasn't expecting much when I took Benny's Gatorade up to the register and said to the girl there, "Got a question. Every hear of a man, Demarest, maybe Walt, used to run a Sunoco here?"

I could see in her eyes how little she knew before she could open her mouth, but a guy down the counter saved her the trouble.

"You mean Vilmer?"

I paid the girl and stepped his way. "Maybe so." I told him about the guy I knew in the seat in the dead-end hallway.

"That's him."

"Family here you know of?"

"Who you exactly?"

I went with a lie that made me sound like a caring geriatric professional, the kind of man who'd have business keeping the Magnolia Hills inmates content.

"Niece," he told me. "Does the books for the Baptists." He pointed more or less at the ceiling. "Name's Mathis. Shirley, I think."

I'll confess it felt good, like old times, teasing a name from a guy, but then I got around to the picnic table where the world went back to normal. Benny had company. A scruffy looking guy on a bike had rolled up and was having a gander at Benny. He was a sight with the leakage and the bib and the mashed up sandwich leavings on the wrapper, and I could tell Benny was already incandescent with indignation. He had the look he gets when somebody needs to be bloodied if not dead.

When I say bike, I don't mean a motorcycle. The guy was perched on the sort of bicycle only a ten-year-old kid or a scruffy lowlife would ride. Banana seat. High rise handlebars. No fenders. Leopard-print frame. He had a spider web tattoo on his near elbow and 'Gloria' in big gothic script inked across his neck. He was all veins and sinew and had probably never shaved in his life but still only had a half inch of scruff.

When he saw me, he did what his sort do and figured I was enough like him that we could share a laugh together. He pointed Benny's way, at Benny's mess, and told me with a chuckle, "Shit."

Benny shot me the look, but I didn't require it. I'd been resigned to slugging the guy from the moment I saw him. If I was going to stand in for Marco, I had to do Marco's brand of stuff, so I caught the boy with a right hand between his eye socket and his ear, threw it leaning in the way you do if you're hoping to throw just the one.

He collapsed with some flair, I'll give him that. He piled up on the pea gravel. His bike fell right on top of him, and Benny started making noises. Knocked out wasn't going to work for Benny. He wanted that boy dead.

"Cop around front." A necessary lie. "Might get complicated."

I wiped Benny down and tidied him up, and we got back into the Chrysler. I already knew there wasn't much hope for the client doomed to follow. He could pay Benny double and put a spit shine on his shoes and still get the knotty end of Benny's dogwood staff. Worse still, it turned out to be a she, anatomically anyway. She'd been what they used to call a woman of easy virtue who'd stayed with it so long that she'd turned into a fleshy lump of neglect.

She was indiscriminately contrary and prickly, which didn't help. She was going to get smacked no matter what she did, but her lip surely worsened and amplified the ordeal for her.

I stayed outside in her front yard — a weedy landfill with mongrels — while Benny behaved like he needed to inside. I heard stuff break. She said a thing. I heard stuff break some more.

Benny finally came out of that woman's house wiping his stick the way he does. I had to hope she was alive still, which seemed likely since she still owed. We headed back south with more Rodelinda. Handel was growing on me by then, and I'd come around from suspecting that Benny was saddled with an affectation once I'd realized I had favorites and even sometimes hummed a bit from Hercules that struck me as lush and sad.

Benny was fine and settled by the time we'd reached our block in Suffolk. I pulled in his drive. We said our goodbyes, and I walked up the road to my house. Gus was sitting at the dinette. She'd had her key a few weeks by then, but I'd always been home when she showed up, so this was the first time she'd used it. She'd brought some brand of tea she liked and was parked there in her t-shirt and panties enjoying a steaming cup. That wasn't necessarily an overture with her. She just didn't care for pants.

I believe I said, "Hey," though possibly not. I could have just sighed and raised an eyebrow.

We'd not started out talking awfully much and had failed to pick up the habit over time.

Whatever I did or might have said, Gus tuned in and understood. She got up, came over, and laid a hand to my cheek, which proved enough to leave me feeling nearly normal and connected — like we had a bond beyond a happenstance meeting at a freezer case.

Homer got past the pneumonia and went back to his smelly, snoring self once they'd taken the tent and the oxygen away. Benny's nephew, Dennis, drove him on Thursdays while Marco did his time, so I kept to my schedule of sitting with Homer for as long as I could stand. Then it was off to the short piece of hallway for me, which stayed empty for a couple of weeks. Mr. Demarest had gotten a bug as well and wasn't wandering the corridors much, so I found out where his room was and went around to see him.

He was low and sleepy, didn't know me at first, and I was making no progress much with him when a woman came in, a proper civilian who proved to be the niece I'd heard about.

"Ms. Mathis?"

She nodded, and I gave her my name. One of my usuals anyway — Bob Raymond. I told her about my Uncle Homer and made him seem more sad than stinky, and then explained how I'd met

Vilmer (I called him) sitting in his spot out in the hall.

"I can't get here as often as I'd like," she said and then stepped to the bed and combed her uncle's hair with her fingers. "Hey, Willy."

And he said, "Eight seven three nine four six slash B."

"He keeps saying that," I said. "What is it?"

"What do you do, Mr. Raymond?"

"I'm a writer." That's what I always tell them because it fits most situations and I can write whatever it seems they need me to have written. I just have to wait and listen and suss out what they require.

"Oh?"

I nodded.

"Of . . . ?"

"All kinds of stuff. That eight seven nine three . . . ?"

"Books?"

"Sometimes."

"It's a file number."

I waited.

"Police file. Right?" She glanced at her uncle. "Girl back home went missing, and Willy took an interest."

"Why's that?"

She had another look at her uncle. "He knew her mother, I think."

I waited some more.

"They found her body. Way out, wasn't it . . ?" Vilmer appeared to be dozing. "In the woods somewhere."

"Sad."

"What kinds of books?"

"Mysteries mostly, but true crime sometimes."

Vilmer Demarest stirred and chimed back in. "Eight seven three nine four six slash B."

"What? You think there's a book in this?" she asked me.

I shrugged. "Could be. Need to know more."

"The stuff's in my garage," she said and turned to her uncle. "Want him to have it?"

Mr Demarest made a phlegmy, quasi-affirmative racket.

"I can swing by some time that's good for you. Bring you a couple of my books if you want."

I even did take her a pair of paperbacks off the shelf in my bedroom. I'd read half of one but hadn't yet opened the other. The novel I'd dipped into was about spies in Prague by a guy whose name was mostly a pile of initials. The other one had a woman on the cover in a bonnet with a knife. I'd be a hack with a raft of pseudonyms, one of those professional typists whose career is given over to cranking out stuff nobody much bothers to read.

From what I could see of her decor, Shirley Mathis preferred Scripture and Southern Living. I was only in the house long enough for her to fetch the garage key and walk me outside. It was more like a car shed really. Plank doors and walls, dirt floor. Mr. Demarest's stuff was stacked in boxes between the back wall and an old Ford tractor. She left me in there to root as I pleased.

I wasn't keen to have a hobby, wasn't hungry for redemption, and I did a fair amount of muttering as I picked through those packing boxes. They were full of the usual stuff of a life that folks let rot but don't throw out. Table clutter, ashtrays, bookends, sauce pans. The man had packed three pressure cookers, a half dozen coffee carafes, and six or eight pairs of squashed dress shoes that had all gone fuzzy with mold. The rest was paperwork and snapshots, safety razors, silk neckties. I climbed up on the tractor to have a rest when I was only halfway through.

"Bob Raymond," I asked myself, "what in God's name are you doing?"

I didn't have any clear idea, and Bob certainly wasn't much help. Years ago I'd been a bad beat cop who'd become a lousy detective. For me, it had finally come down to a decent pension or a racketeering indictment, so I never saw the light and got anything like clean but only took my money and got out. There was no learning for me and precious little regret. I was bad at the start and bad at the end and had no feelings at all of nostalgia, which left me to wonder on that tractor seat what I was doing in that shed.

I found the file. Big fat thing full of copies of police documents, badly xeroxed photos, and scraps of spiral notepaper that Vilmer Demarest (I decided) had scrawled all over. There was a placemat from a diner, a freezer bag with a necklace in it, and a legal envelope half full of dirt.

Mr. Mathis was home by the time I got finished. He was taking the edge off his day with a beer, and when I tapped on the door to tell Shirley goodbye, she insisted I come in. She gave her husband an abbreviated Bob Raymond biography. He had the look of one of those men who couldn't generate much interest in anything that came out of his wife's mouth.

"Right," he said. "You done then?"

I nodded and showed them both the accordion file I intended to take.

"He visits Willy. Don't you?"

I nodded.

"Probably make a book out of this."

The husband had a snort for that.

I carried all that paperwork home and then couldn't be bothered to go through it. That accordion file sat on the floor by my sofa for probably three solid weeks. I drove Benny. I visited Homer. Gus showed up every few days and scratched on my screen door like a cat.

I didn't say anything the first time she arrived bruised. People knock into stuff out in the world, and sometimes it leaves a mark.

Then she stripped out of her trousers one day and had a blue/black on her thigh. That one I asked her to account for, and she told me, "Jeremy junior has moods."

The third one was a clear handprint on her shoulder and the side of her neck. I'd seen no end of that sort of thing back when I was policing. It was a power play sometimes but more often general aggravation accumulated and bursting out. A man takes crap at work for a solid week, reaches his outer limit, and then comes home and shoves his wife, maybe smacks her once or twice.

With the pressure relieved, they both reset and recalibrate a bit. He resolves to be kinder to her (or at least expand his outer limit) while she thinks of painful ways to kill him in due time. His new tolerance for more crap leads to a promotion, while she buys and learns to use a gun. It's one of those bad dynamics that never quite gets fixed.

I took a good look at Gus' bruise. "Big Jeremy?"

She had a boys-will-be-boys short of shrug and used it on me.

I didn't for a moment suspect big Jeremy was ripe for a life lesson since I doubt most grownups can hope to evolve and change, but I figured a dose of aversion therapy might be just the thing to reach him and persuade him he could be well-behaved or dead.

I turned to Benny for advice and help. "Got any female muscle?" I asked him.

I knew Benny to be open-minded, a culturally progressive sort, so if there was a capable, vicious woman for hire, Benny would know it and probably had used her. He was even further along with that and named three straightaway.

"Wendy," he told me. "Judo or something. Can't hope to lay a finger on her. She's butch, though. Spiky hair, tats. She'd put you down so fast you wouldn't know she was a girl. C.C.'s more the sniper type."

"Got to be up close," I said. "Girly girl would help."

"Carla. Did the octagon for a couple of years. Her ears look like hell, but she lets her hair hang down."

"A puncher? A kicker? Choke them out?"

Benny smiled and told me, "Yeah."

He put us together. I met Carla outside a
Walgreen's where I showed her the photo I'd
taken of Gus' bruise. She was feminine enough
from a reasonable distance, but she looked like
your little brother in a wig up close.

"Don't want him going after her," I explained.
"He needs to think the sisterhood'll find him out
and put him down."

Carla nodded. She named her price and had me
text her Gus' photo.

"Where and when?" she asked me.

I gave her a couple of possibilities. "Wear
something pretty," I said.

She pretended to hit me. I wasn't pretending to
flinch.

I didn't see it happen, just got an after action.
Carla caught him coming out of the Best Buy in
the middle of the day. She pulled out her phone
and showed Jeremy the picture I'd taken of Gus'
bruise, and then she struck him twice in tender
places before showing it to him again.

"Slow to catch on," she told me.

"What did he say?"

"Ouch. Don't. The usual."

Big Jeremy looked the same on the outside.
That was the beauty of a professional like Carla.
She was advocating for a point of view with an
audience of one. Jeremy needed to be persuaded

without ending up looking broken. That's where the skill comes in since any fool can knock a guy unconscious, just bang on his head hard enough, and he's sure to go. Carla knew where the soft bits were and the most efficient way to reach them.

I could tell she'd been successful when Gus came over a few days after with no fresh marks and no apparent idea her Jeremy had been thumped.

"How's things?" I asked her as innocently as I could manage.

Not innocently enough apparently. "What's with you?"

"Nothing."

Then, luckily for me, Gus noticed the accordion folder I'd moved to the floor in the dead spot between my sofa and my hassock.

"What's this?"

"Doing something for a guy."

I tried to get by with vague hand-waving, but Gus lifted the flap and pulled out a few glossies of a dead girl half covered with leaves.

"Old case I'm looking into."

"You some kind of cop?"

I shook my head. "Just nosy."

She plucked out the grimmest forensic photo. Teeth and bone and rotted skin. I filled her in on Vilmer Demarest in his dead-end piece of hall.

Gus sifted through some of the documents, checked a date on a witness statement.

"2004?"

I nodded. "Real whodunnit."

"You going to find out what happened?"

"Probably not."

This was more than we'd talked to each other in the course of the previous month.

"I'm good with puzzles and stuff." She pulled out more photos.

We heard the secret knock, and Gus was the one to shout out, "Come on in."

Dwight was accustomed by then to seeing Gus in her underpants. Since she was probably crowding forty, she only barely registered for him as a female. I fetched Dwight's fresh twelve pack and handed it over.

"Cold case," Gus said, waving pages from the file. "Want to work it?"

"Come on," I told her. "Nothing to work."

"Yeah. Maybe. I guess," Dwight said.

"You out of cheerleaders?" I asked him.

Gus pointed at herself. "Brains." She pointed at Dwight. "IT." I was good for "legwork and stuff."

Gus seemed excited and interested, so who was I to bark.

By then she was clutching that nasty, mildewed accordion file to her chest, like it was a favorite pillow or a first husband.

iii

The first rule was that Dwight couldn't upload the ghoulish forensic photos and broadcast them to all his chatty teenage friends. The second rule was that breaking the first rule meant no more beer for Dwight, and third rule (apparently) was that I had to buy everything Gus and Dwight decided we needed. Whiteboard, a corkboard, assorted markers and all manner of push pins because it took me four tries to purchase the brand my colleagues found useful and worthy.

They set up the command center in my extra bedroom while, for my part, I planted myself on the sofa and worked through every page of the file.

I was hardly a quarter of the way into it before the case felt hopeless to me. Norfolk PD and the Greene County sheriff's office had handled the murder jointly. They'd only ever identified a pair of suspects, and one of them was six years dead. The other had an alibi, backed up with a trio of affidavits, and the victim, Ms. Tucker, looked squeaky clean and blameless on the page. No drug history and hardly the type of girl known to consort with bad actors.

She'd been at home in Chuckatuck, as far as anybody could say, before she got reported missing and (two years later) turned up dead in a glorified ditch in a national park one hundred and forty miles away.

"So?" Gus asked me on the first break I took.

I gave her the stack of stuff I'd read. "Sure glad you're the brains."

Gus and Dwight seemed to think we'd solve the case and identify the killer just by sifting through the contents of that musty file. As far as they were concerned, the clues we needed were in a photo, on a page, and we'd be savvy enough to notice the crumbs and string them all together because we were a decade more modern and tuned in than the cops at the time had been.

They kept staring at the whiteboard, most particularly at the dead girl who, by the time a hunter found her, was bones and teeth and scraps of rotted clothing. There were pictures of her various parts alongside a bright yellow wooden ruler, all of them taken in a clinically lit forensic lab. The photos were crisp and ghastly, certainly precise. You knew that bit of upper arm with some dried meat clinging to it was an inch and a quarter across and almost seven inches long, but that didn't really help, and Gus and Dwight got more than a little deflated when the case nobody had figured out left them stymied too.

For my part, I was working pretty full on and so had a ready distraction. They'd come in while I was out, and I'd show up once they'd both left. I'd find documents shifted around, photos regrouped, witness statements highlighted. They'd have a browse, get an idea, raise a question on the whiteboard, think better of it and wipe the thing clean, start the whole business afresh.

I stayed busy driving where Benny told me, listening to Handel, mashing up lunch, and then making my Thursday visits to Magnolia Hills. Vilmer Demarest had soon recovered enough to return to his chair in the hall, and I sought him out and tried to pump him for whatever he might know.

We always had to start the same way. He'd say, "Hey, listen." I'd say, "Abigail Tucker," and he'd come back with "Eight seven three nine four six slash B". It was like our Masonic handshake. It couldn't not be done.

Vilmer still had bits of the file's contents lodged in his head, but they weren't in any particular order, not ranked by value and use, just morsels that had stayed with him and cropped up however they wanted. He knew the map coordinates, for instance, the latitude and longitude of the spot where Abigail Tucker's body was found. I know it now too since I heard it enough — 38.29 north by 78.62 west.

'Colby' was another one. That name kept bubbling up, and I knew him to be the junior detective from Norfolk on the case. I got a rise out of Vilmer with a ratty evidence tag that we'd been puzzling over, which Gus had plucked out from the bottom of the file. It looked official, was marked Greene County SD, and there were a couple of scrawled lines of commentary or description or something, but the writing was faded and had been sloppy to start with, so we couldn't work it out.

"Remember this?" I asked him and offered the tag.

It was tan, foxed card stock with a rotted string tie. He took it from me and held it, closed his waxy fingers around it.

There was a number stenciled on the back. "Three nine double deuce four," he told me. He hadn't needed to see it to get it right.

I waited for more, but it didn't come.

"What does that go with?" I asked him.

"Hey, listen."

I groaned. We sat in silence for a while.

Vilmer fixed on the shiny, red fire alarm box directly across the hall.

I was about to give up when he opened his hand. "Silver plate," he told me. "Winking crescent moon." He added, "Barrel Point," and dropped that tag onto the floor.

I knew Barrel Point. It was maybe eight miles east of Chuckatuck where the black top dead ended at the bay. It had been trashy marshland for a long time but had lately gotten reclaimed. The houses out there were new and large, situated on piney waterfront lots with views across towards Hampton.

I rode out and took a few photos with my phone, got challenged by a lady in a golf cart. It was her day to make visitors feel unwelcome, and she did a fine job of it. She was sour and suspicious, opened with a threat. I was under surveillance — she pointed out the cameras — and they already had my license number and so knew where to scoop me up.

"For what?"

"You know." She pointed generally at everything the way Haile Selassie might. It was all hers, theirs, most certainly not mine.

As I was getting back in my car, I said to her, "Abigail Tucker. Mean anything?"

"Tuckers! No!" It was quite a reaction. She did everything but spit.

I came home to an empty house, just me and my command center where I attached that ratty evidence tag to the corkboard with a push pin.

Dwight, Gus, or both together had rearranged everything again and written all kinds of speculative stuff on the whiteboard in red marker. I turned the accordion file upside down and shook it over the spare room rug in hopes a winking half moon charm would drop out at my feet. Instead I got three dead silverfish and two paper clips.

Gus swung by for at most a quarter hour and kept her trousers on. "Had an idea," she told me and made a note on the whiteboard next to a mugshot of a warty woman. It was some brief bit of business about Graves disease that Gus mostly kept to herself.

"Lost Dwight for a few days," she said. "Something about a . . . client?"

That's how Dwight usually referred to girls from his school who were plagued with social network regret and needed him to tinker with the evidence against them.

"Pep Squad," I explained to Gus. "Dwight revirginates them ."

Things stalled out for us the way I knew they would. Cases don't go cold for nothing. Dwight had printed out some newspaper copy from The Times-Dispatch, The Virginian-Pilot, The Winchester Star, The Suffolk-News Herald. I'd worked homicides where we knew who did it but couldn't muster an indictment, but the reporting on this one was all over the place. If the cops had their eye on somebody for real, they sure didn't let it out. Two persons of interest — one dead, one in Ohio during the crime.

"Dry hole," I told the whiteboard and the mug of markers, and then Benny called and had me drive him to visit Marco in jail.

We took Marco pepperoni, the pre-sliced kind in pouches, and two boxes of the brand of rye toast cracker Marco ate out in the world. We sat with him at a metal table in the county lockup visitor's room where inmates, for the most part, were either holding hands and leaning close against their women or hearing sharply about all the stuff they'd made worse by getting their asses locked up.

Marco was married, but his wife and kids lived most of the year at their place in Boca Chica. She'd come over for a week or two here and there when Marco, I guess, was flush or needy, but she wasn't the sort of creature who was about to visit him in jail.

I brought Marco a copy of David Copperfield because he wasn't allergic to reading and was kind of a wry and funny sort when he wasn't behind a slow car.

He opened the book and had a peek. "I am born," Marco said.

Benny tried to give him money for his canteen account or something, but Marco wouldn't take it. He had pepperoni and crackers, a book to read. He was fine. Benny wasn't there because he was worried that Marco might be loose-lipped and unreliable but because Benny had a decent streak that didn't involve his dogwood staff. He cared about Marco, even cared about me a little, which isn't to say he wouldn't throttle us given cause, but Benny plainly had a spot that wasn't rough and mercenary. That was the guy I drove for, what I told myself anyway. The one Handel touched, the Benny who often asked about my uncle, the Benny who read the culture pages of the Wall Street Journal. The Benny who thanked me when his sandwiches got mashed.

Thinking about him that way reminded me of an old cop lesson, the sort of thing you don't know when you start out and that it's easy to forget. It doesn't, I learned, take wretched people to do evil, nasty things — I'm talking homicides here, like leaving a dead teen to rot in a shallow crease in the woods. It's usually just the wretched ones who repeat that sort of business. Abigail Tucker might have run across a guy on his solitary, homicidal day, and then he went back to work and home and church, went back to ordinary. That's why cases get cold. You're looking for a killer who doesn't, in any practical sense, exist.

For me, those were the scary sorts, the folks who did something feral and then picked up their normal lives and lead them like nothing had changed. Sitting there listening to Benny and Marco and smelling the sweaty lockup smells, I remembered a case, a bludgeoning. The doer insisted we call him Avery and was the type who always rose to his feet and tried to shake your hand.

Avery sold auto parts and covered a territory that stretched from Baltimore to Bridgeport. He had a house and a wife and a spaniel in Allentown or somewhere, and he'd killed a man at a derelict shopping plaza outside Frederick, Maryland, a Sikh in a turban which, given the climate at the time, looked like some kind of pinhead, anti-Arab thing.

The case went unsolved for nearly four years. They had DNA off the body but nothing to match it to until Avery got swabbed for a drunk driving stop. He and the wife were coming from a

Christmas do where they'd put rum in the punch. He told us all about it and was embarrassed, apologetic. Me and my partner and been asked to pick him up at one of our local Napa stores.

"This is something else," I explained. I named the date, the shopping plaza. Identified the murdered Sikh.

Avery said (I'll never forget it), "Oh, that."

He couldn't tell us why he'd killed the guy. I got the feeling he couldn't remember, but if I'd beat a man to pulpy death with a chunk of concrete, I believe I'd have some lingering idea why. Avery supposed it had been a misunderstanding, and that's about all he would say except for wondering if we'd phone his wife and tell her he might be delayed.

"I'm due home Thursday," Avery said like he'd fit us in as long as he could.

He might have beaten a man to death, but he'd not allowed it to stain him. His conscience wasn't burdened. It was just a thing that happened, and he'd closed it off so completely that it hardly registered anymore. He didn't seem for even a passing moment to think there'd be consequences.

The version Avery gave us of the killing had no useful details to it, but I feel certain he wasn't being evasive. He simply couldn't recall them.

"A misunderstanding, I'm sure," he kept saying. Then he'd rap the table with his knuckles and smile our way as if to ask, "We good?"

Avery's wife knew to be disgusted and appalled. She shrieked at him in the courtroom as the judge was accepting his plea, and I remember the look on Avery's face. He appeared embarrassed for her. Why all the drama? Sure he'd beat a man to death, but only just the once.

Avery was precisely the sort you ruled out when you'd decided you were looking for a monster, but Avery was still the devil, just precious little of the time, and I feared there was an Avery in 873946/ B, some guy who'd done an awful thing and then gone straight back to normal.

"Tuckers?," I asked Benny. "Barrel Point? Every run across any?"

"Not anymore. Seen that place?"

I nodded. "Pretty nice."

We were listening to Tamerlano (not one of my favorites) and heading to pay a call on a serial delinquent, a gambling addict up by Benns Church who always required incentive.

"Ten, fifteen years ago, maybe," Benny told me, "Tuckers out there like rats."

"They a bad sort?"

Benny gave it some thought. He was uncommonly careful, as a rule, about the levels of human worthlessness. Most of Benny's customers were challenged — that was the word he liked to use — when it came to basic questions of moral decency, but Benny was loath to lump the ones who simply pilfered and stole to get ahead in with the crowd that would do far worse and not sweat the details much.

He shook his head. "Just trash," he said. Then Benny fell silent in that thoughtful way that always made me uneasy. "Sunoco? Tuckers? What are you up to?"

I thought it best to tell him something like the truth, so I laid it out briefly. "Abigail Tucker," I finally told him. "Would have been 2002."

"Found her in the woods, a lot later, right?"

I nodded. "Two years."

"I remember. She wasn't one of them. Not really."

She had been, as it turned out, an authentic Barrel Point Tucker, but her parents had both died on her — one out in the world from leukemia and the other shivved at Dillwyn Correctional — and she got taken in by a Christian couple who'd never had children of their own.

"Kennards," Benny told me. "I knew them a little. Bought a couple of cars from him. Don't think I met the girl."

"Ever hear talk of who killed her?" It was worth a shot. If anybody would know, it'd be Benny.

Benny shook his head. "What's your end?"

"Just curious."

That got a laugh.

"Man at the old folks home. It's eating him up. Kind of told him I'd take a look."

Benny pointed. "Left up here. Park at the dumpster."

That's what I did, and then he indicated the back of the house just past a hedgerow. "Knock on the front door. Say 'Police' or something. He'll come slipping around here."

It was a brick ranch with an extraordinary range of crap in the yard. There was a path through the hedgerow that led to a trash heap not ten yards from the dumpster. Beyond that sat a Chevy that would never see the road again. Then a pile of ladder-back chairs, a couple of cracked and sun-bleached kiddie pools, a stack of car batteries, an overturned mower, about sixty percent of a wheelbarrow, but the junk all quit in the side yard. The front lawn was a decent-people facade. Trimmed shrubbery. Clipped grass. A lone tricycle by way of clutter.

I went straight up onto the small front porch and pounded on the door.

"Sheriff's department."

I waited a quarter minute and did it all again. The front door shifted slightly as the back door, I guess, flew open, and by the time I'd passed through the hedgerow again Benny was deep into informing his client that he'd become more delinquent than Benny could see fit to allow.

It was part talk and part dogwood. The client was on his back like a bug, and Benny was holding him down with a foot and tapping him when he felt like it. The guy just nodded and swallowed and closed his eyes, took his lumps in relative silence. He knew he was behind with Benny, and he was aware of what that meant.

This kind of thing didn't bother me. Everybody had a part, and they played it. The client didn't appear to blame me for driving him out of his house. Benny bruised him a fair bit but chose not to break the skin. He needed the guy to pass for normal and go out and be an earner. It was the sort of scene, if you walked up on it, would look worse than it was.

The client promised to make his payment. Benny gave him an extra two days. Once I got the nod, I helped the guy up. He wasn't much rattled. He thanked me. Then me and Benny climbed back into the Chrysler and headed east for Wakefield. Benny had me switch to Jeptha, and he opened his WSJ again.

I'd picked up the Wakefield payment for him and was passing it over the seatback, when Benny asked me out the blue (a tactic he was fond of), "Who exactly's the lady with no the pants?"

Benny didn't miss much. I'd beat him to the question but not by an awful lot. It had hit me, maybe a week before, that I didn't know much about Gus. I was aware she shopped at Trader Joe's and got smacked around occasionally. She took Jeremy junior to kid stuff. He had drum lessons and played league soccer. Big Jeremy made mid six figures doing something or another. Gus drove a pale green Volvo wagon and drank some kind of smokey tea.

That wasn't enough to satisfy me, so I followed her home one afternoon to see exactly where she lived and how. Sleepy Cove, as it turned out, on a cul-de-sac between a finger of the Chesapeake and a golf course. Her place made the McMansions at Barrel Point seem like the pretentious trash they were. She had a proper Dutch colonial on probably a full acre with a boat dock, a side-yard fountain, a three-car garage, a putting green.

I'd laid back to keep inconspicuous, but Gus had seen me anyway. Once she'd parked in her drive, she came walking straight out to my car.

"Happy?"

I took in the splendor. "Not really. What the hell does he do?"

Gus shrugged. "Something with mortgages. Got a head for it. Want the tour?"

"How are your closet rods?"

"Flaccid."

"Guess I'll pass."

She turned and headed back towards her driveway.

"Hey," I called out, "when did you see me?"

Gus just snorted, so probably from the start.

~ ~ ~

Homer died at half past three on a Thursday morning, and they called me from Magnolia Hills to tell me straightaway.

"He yielded in his sleep," the woman told me. More stink, less snoring.

I didn't rush over but drove out at my regular time since it was my day for Magnolia Hills anyway. They'd put Homer's stuff in a box that jugs of ammonia had come in, just his table clutter and the few books he'd brought in with him. His pajamas had all ended up in a garbage bag, which seemed fitting. They were cleaning his room when I got there, every inch, even scrubbing the walls, and one of the guys directed me to a room down in the basement where the residents got stored before the funeral home came.

Homer had company down there, three other Magnolia Hillers under sheets. The man in charge uncovered Homer halfway down and then discreetly retired so I could have a moment with my uncle. I'm not religious. We weren't close. So I just stood there in silence and endured one of those way-of-all-flesh sensations like I guess most people would.

I signed papers and sent my uncle off with the mortuary men and then went back upstairs for his box of stuff. I found Mr. Demarest where he usually was and told him about Homer, but the shiny, red fire alarm had hold of him by then.

"Abigail Tucker."

That snagged his attention. He shifted around to make a noise my way and give me a squinty look.

"I went to Barrel Point," I said. "It's all big houses now."

He looked neither surprised nor disappointed. It could be he hadn't even heard me. He told me something back, but it was mostly phlegm.

"What was that?"

"Colby." I heard it this time

"Norfolk cop."

He grunted. "Kennard."

"Her . . . parents." That was close enough. They'd taken her in when she was twelve.

Wilmer nodded, watched the candy-red alarm box, eventually told me, "Hey, listen."

I didn't seek out the Kennards and try to locate Colby straightway, didn't think I had the material yet to interview them to much effect and couldn't be sure I ever would. Dwight stayed busy with the pep squad and Gus went on a boat trip with her husband, one of those Danube cruises that started in Munich and went to Budapest.

"Just the two of us. Christ," she told me. Junior was staying with his aunt.

"Might get that spark back."

Gus didn't look amused. "Might go over the rail and drown."

I felt a twinge of jealousy (I guess), but it didn't last. I decided to read and do a bit of a clean out while Gus was gone, by which I meant Trollope and a week's worth of soup and salad to set my internals right.

Homer's passing hit me harder than I ever thought it would. It was more the idea of him being dead than any surprise at his actual dying. Everybody else was gone already, so he'd left me the last of the lot, and I felt it far more than I'd expected, wasn't the sort who usually felt much.

The funeral home put the service together, posted the notices, even wrote the obit, but I still figured on being alone in the chapel since I'd seen no evidence that Homer had any friends. He'd been prickly as hell in his regular life before he went to sleep, so when I showed up for the service, I was surprised to find a rather fashionable looking woman in the chapel. Maybe seventy-five by the looks of her and leggy and sleek and dressed to the nines.

A clergyman talked. He'd not known Homer. He worked for the mortuary but was practiced at paying tribute to people he'd never actually met. The man had a knack for plucking the strings just so. He reminded me a bit of Benny without the CP slosh and slur. The preacher called me out by name (I was paying the bill after all), and he invited me up to throw the switch that sent Homer into the furnace.

The man closed with a prayer and then offered his soft, moist hand to me for a shake. The lady who'd come was nearly outside before I managed to catch her.

"Excuse me," I said. She stopped and turn. "You knew Homer?"

"Oh, yes."

We introduced ourselves. Marjorie was all I got from her.

"Are you his friend from out west . . . and Newport News?"

"It's rather complicated." She shifted like she was ready to leave.

"He's the last of my bunch," I told her. "I'd sure like to know more than I do."

We ended up at a Chinese buffet in a nearby shopping plaza. I got a plate of fried rice and lo mien just to shut the waiter up. She wasn't, as it turned out, the lady friend I'd heard of but was a woman Homer had fallen for once he got to Newport News.

"I knew Helen," she told me.

"She the one from Idaho?"

Marjorie nodded. "You never met her?"

"I barely knew Homer. He was my mother's little brother. They fell out."

"I played canasta with Helen. Met him that way. We ended up having . . . a thing."

A thing with Homer? This woman? She might have been pushing eighty, but she was clearly a thoroughbred. The type with cheekbones and all the right proportions. Her dress was sleeveless because she still had guns, and her eyes were a pale and arresting shade of green.

"You and Homer?" That came out sounding more skeptical and flabbergasted than I wanted.

"He was fascinating, and I can be weak. Helen was my friend."

"She still around?"

Marjorie shook her head and left it at that.

"What happened with you and him?"

"My husband disapproved."

"They'll do that."

"We had an understanding, but he drew the line at Homer."

I had to go with the husband on this one. She stood up. I did as well.

The waiter swooped in. "You finish?" He all but threw the bill my way.

I passed most of that evening in the command center back home, eyeing our whiteboard and chewing on the case. Dwight had turned up several photos of Abigail Tucker in life. She'd been strawberry blonde and freckled, given to baby fat. She'd become an active Church of Christer thanks (I had to think) to the Kennards. In three of the photos, she wore a crucifix, but there was no record of it having been found. No charm bracelet either, just the evidence tag. She'd been found with fourteen dollars in her pocket and her some kind of school ID along with a plastic ring on her finger made to look like a black-eyed Susan. The Kennards insisted they'd never seen the thing before.

I decided to do what I always did when I was stuck or stymied. I decided to change the angle, come at the thing from the other end.

On the Pull

i

Simmons Gap is nowhere, just a dip in the terrain, probably a spot where the locals used to make their way over the Blue Ridge mountains. I timed my trip from Chuckatuck, and it was three hours and change in light traffic on a Sunday morning.

There's a Simmons Gap ranger station, but you have to go into the park to reach it. For me, that meant driving up a gravel track north of a place called Mission Home, a road that climbed into the forest a ways and then quit at steel posts and a chain. It was little more than a footpath from there on up, which carried me clear to the Skyline Drive. That's where I checked my GPS and started homing in on the spot.

It was a rare piece of luck the poor girl even got found. The place was wild and desolate, just a crease below a rocky ledge where a logging road had probably run. I toed around in the leaf litter, like you do, idly and expecting nothing. I got something close to that, found two lobes of a plastic lily that I could imagine those Kennards leaving as a kind of remembrance for their girl.

Then I walked up to the ranger station, a modest frame building off a spur of the road in the woods with a secluded gravel lot. About as perfect a place as you could find for shifting corpses.

I had turned up an address for the Greene County sheriff, many years retired, so I headed over towards Stanardsville and located the house I was after. There was a big, wheezy man out in the yard with a hose. Filling his birdbath. Washing his sidewalk. Squirting off his bay window. He stood in the same spot and did it all.

I parked in his ditch. He glanced my way and then went back to squirting.

"Mr. Foley?"

He was in no hurry to answer me. "That's right."

I told him what I was up to, mentioned Vilmer Demarest by name. The guy groaned and asked me, "He still kicking?"

"Oh yeah."

"You run a gas station too?"

"No, sir. I used to be a cop."

That led to an exchange of pedigrees.

"What do you want?"

"Got any better ideas now than you had back then?"

He dropped the hose. The nozzle hit the sidewalk and squirted us both a little. Mr. Foley was about three hundred pounds of ex-sheriff on the hoof, and he shifted towards a nearby poplar tree to steady himself against it.

Maybe he did some thinking. He did some wheezing anyway before he shook his head and told me, "Naw."

"Never had a decent suspect?"

"Read the file?"

I nodded.

"You see one?"

I shook my head.

"Two we liked weren't mean enough for that."

"You sure?"

He nodded. "I always thought it was probably somebody passing through."

That's the rural lawman fallback when stuff's too ugly for one of their own.

"So nobody stands out?"

Foley shook his head. "And it isn't like I haven't thought some on it."

"What about the boy who found her?"

"What about him?"

"He still around? Think I could talk to him?"

"Who you again?"

I went through it all with what charm I could muster and a smile.

"Let me make a call," he told me and shoved off from his tree.

The boy who found Abigail Tucker half rotted in the woods was a Blaylock who managed a Tractor Supply store in the town of Orange. He had given himself a Sunday shift and was at the register when I came in. He'd been warned to expect me, and he let me join him for his cigarette break on a slab of concrete just through the back door. The store was pretty much out in the country with a view across a stubbled corn field of one of those rural suburbs where the trees had all been shoved down and the houses all slapped up.

He smoked a Merit as we talked. Then a second one, and a third one, all sucked on hard and hooded with his hand.

"They tell you they wrote me a ticket?" That was about the first thing he said.

"For what?"

"Hunting in the park. Eight hundred and seventy-five dollars."

"Who wrote it?"

"Ranger."

I'd read the file closely. I didn't recall a ranger figuring in. "He got a name?"

"Randy fucking Pyle." Blaylock drew hard on his butt.

"Did you know him from before?"

He shook his head. "And I ain't paid it yet."

I pulled out my ratty notebook and made an actual note. Randy Pyle.

"Mind telling me about that day?"

He made a noise in his neck and then started. "Flat place in the woods. I saw this yellow thing. In the leaves, you know? February the twelfth, 2002." He stopped talking for a bit after that and smoked with more violence than before. I waited. I might have always been a middling to lousy cop, but I'd long had a gift for leaving a gap alone.

He showed me his finger. "Turned out to be her ring. Flower on it. A daisy. Big plastic thing."

I nodded and made like I was doing some jotting.

"Moved the leaves a little, and there she was."

"What did you do?"

Blaylock looked at me like I was simple. He called the law. He told them about her.

"I mean what did you do first? Walk me through it."

"Had my rifle, so I thought twice and all, but I went up to the ranger station. Figured he'd have a phone. Long time ago, you know? Ain't like it is now with . . . stuff."

"So Randy Pyle called it in?"

He nodded.

"First cops on the scene?"

"Foley and them. Figured out who she was —
had stuff in her pockets. They called Norfolk or
somewhere. I told them all I knew, five or six
times over, and that was it."

"Keep up with the case?"

"From the paper. Sad thing, kid like that."

"Been reading the file," I said. "No Randy Pyle
in it. Sure about him?"

"Yep."

He'd had enough of me. Blaylock flicked his
butt and went back inside, left me to make my
way around the building, past the kennels and the
galvanized cow troughs, the mowers and the
garden tillers, all laced through with steel cable so
you'd have to steal the lot.

The first Randy Pyle I turned up on my phone
owned a smoothie shop in Tallahassee. He was
toothy and tan and sported a high-lit architectural
haircut and looked a very long way from upland
ranger stock.

So Gus was on the Danube. I was Googling in
Orange, while Dwight was probably either tidying
up some pep squader's errant upload or enjoying
a solid two minutes of unimpassioned gratitude.
Weren't we a crack investigative force.

I read my Trollope and ate my romaine, gave up
lager for vodka for a bit, and showed up promptly

at Benny's down the block every morning at half
past eight. He'd lately come into an owner's share
of a gentleman's club (they called it) down near
the Norfolk shipyard. Benny had taken the piece
as collateral, and then the client had skipped out
and gone too far away to bother finding.

The neighborhood was strip joint territory, but
that gentleman's club had ambitions thanks
primarily to the brothers who oversaw the place
day-to-day and spent way too much time fussing
with the decor and the menu.

"Why would you come down here to eat?"
Benny asked them. "And what's with all the
sconces?"

I was just standing by waiting for them to
answer Benny when the plumper one, let's call
him Carson (I never could quite fix on their actual
names) pointed at Benny and asked me, "What
exactly's up with him?"

I'd been around Benny long enough by then
that he sounded normal to me. He was a wet
talker on account of his CP, and he could slur and
swallow his words, but I'd never found him
difficult to decipher. I doubt those boys did
either, but they were the sort who needed to point
this planet's lesser creatures out. They had hair
and teeth and squandered educations while

Benny was compromised and damaged which Carson felt the need to advertise.

I would have turned away if Benny had given me the time to do it. He caught Carson square in the forehead with the knobby end of his dogwood staff. The skin split and blood flowed, and Carson's brother got irate. Miles maybe. Lacrosse midfielder with a few too many single malts under his belt. He objected. He closed, and Benny whacked him just behind the ear. First Miles look surprised, then disappointed, then invertebrate.

The staff failed to rise to their defense. You had to figure Carson and Miles had insulted all of them by then. The bartender kept to his business and just watched the brothers bleed. The bouncer on hand, a beefy black guy with hieroglyphs carved into his hair, sized up the situation and went back to watching the door. The girls around screamed a little at first but opted soon enough for giggling instead.

I rustled up a rag for Carson to hold against his forehead. He was flowing like a spigot with blood coursing into his eyes and dripping steadily off his chin. Miles was chiefly bruised and addled and kept telling himself mostly, "Ow."

"Listen up," Benny said. "Burgers. Two of them. Right there."

Benny pointed at a table in the far corner, and I followed him over to it. This was a test, Benny explained to me. Strip clubs were burgers and nipples and beers. "You don't gussy it up."

I knew just what he meant, but Miles and Carson needed a lesson. They were proud of their Kobe burger with Morbier cheese and celeriac coleslaw, their shoestring sweet potatoes with just a hint of truffle oil, and all of it for a princely eighteen dollars.

It was tasty stuff but wrong for a shipyard joint, which was the message Benny meant to deliver, and he'd hammer it in any way he could.

"He's taking over." Benny pointed at me.

I hadn't guessed that was coming. I'd dated a stripper once but only for a weekend when she gave my keys to her real boyfriend and he stole and sold my car.

"Who is he exactly?" Carson, I think, was doing the talking.

"Your boss," Benny explained.

Miles jerked his brother's sleeve and said, "I think my brain is bleeding."

Even once we were back in the Chrysler, I didn't say anything at first. I just found Benny in the mirror and waited for him to find me back.

"What am I supposed to do?" I asked him.

"Educate those two," he said.

That turned out to be a challenge. Carson and Miles knew how to be snotty and defensive better than they knew anything else. They were UVA grads. Alden loafers. Madras shorts, even and especially in the winter. The chef was one of their school mates and so was like them but with a marginal skill. They had a tuna dish on the menu that they'd decided was their line in the sand, lightly charred Ahi loin just like they'd eaten one time at some swanky place on Kapahula Ave.

I believe it was Miles who explained to me, "That'd be in Hawaii."

Instead of hitting him, I explained back that we were all in Norfolk. "And not even nice Norfolk."

He snorted, so I tapped his Adam's apple, did it only medium hard and just the once.

Miles made the kazoo noise you want, right between regular breathing and death. I pulled out a chair and put him on it. Carson came up on me all shirty, so I tapped him as well. Cooking school, I guess, had broken their chef friend who just showed me his palms and smiled.

The hostess ducked over to check on us. That's right, our gentleman's club had a hostess, a girl named Raven, a pretty, flat-chested thing in a tasteful cocktail dress. She was haughty and inattentive and had slept with Carson or Miles or both. Raven didn't dance. She hung out at the end of the bar and answered the phone, usually on about the twelfth ring.

I hauled Carson and Miles and the chef around the corner to a diner where I made them eat fish sticks and patty melts. The prices were right. The staff was efficient. The beer was PBR or Yuengling, and not served ironically or with a glass.

"Got it?" I asked them.

They all three nodded.

"You make changes or Benny comes back."

Then we closed for two days and opened fresh, put up posters on the local light posts and flyers in shop windows. We gave away hot dogs, had screwed red light bulbs into most of the sconces, brought in a special act from Atlantic City — a trio of scary looking girls who took precisely zero shit. Folks turned out, and they were all the right sort, lots of blue collar hard heads with crumpled cash money and wives who knew exactly where they were and didn't care.

Carson and Miles canned their buddy, the Ahi chef, once they got a look at the take.

For a stretch there, I worked from noon to midnight. Benny used his cousin, Dennis, to drive him while I coaxed and flogged the last scraps unhelpful ambition out of Carson and Miles. That didn't leave me much time at home, but nothing was going on there anyway until I rolled up one afternoon and found Gus and Dwight on duty. She was back from the Danube, and Dwight had tidied the pep squad up.

"Hi team," I told them.

Dwight looked his usual pimply self, but Gus seemed irritatingly refreshed.

She was downright perky. "Miss us?"

"No time. Been running a strip club for a couple of weeks."

Dwight's breathing changed. I think he told me or the universe or somebody, "Wow."

Naturally, they wanted to visit the place, have a burger, see the girls — and solve, if Dwight could manage it, the odd tech problem (and we had a few). I took them at three in the afternoon on a Tuesday when I knew there'd be a lull. Carson greeted us at the front door. His forehead was healing nicely, and he walked us to a prime corner table while getting chatted up by Gus.

Dwight had an involved conversation with Tammy, a Richmond girl you wouldn't look at twice with all her clothes on, but she had the flair and the flash to rattle men in her spangly underthings. Attitude is most of it. No missing front teeth helps. Tammy had some kind of iPad problem and took Dwight back into the dressing room so he could do some tech magic for her and meet a few of her friends.

Our burgers were inoffensive, and our fries were crisp. "Coffee any good here?" Gus wanted to know. I directed her attention to the buffed chrome of Miles and Carson's espresso machine, an investment they'd made before Benny had come around with his dogwood corrective.

Our double shots came with demerara sugar and a couple of salted caramel wafers.

"Fancy," Gus said.

I nodded. "Kind of the problem."

We'd come over in Gus' Volvo. I let Dwight have the front going back so I could be spared the wonders of Tammy and the side excursion devoted to her willowy friend Anette.

They beat me up some about Simmons Gap, especially once I'd owned up to talking to the sheriff and that Blaylock. "Still need to find a ranger," I told them.

"Got a name?" Dwight asked me.

"Randy Pyle."

Dwight went after him on his phone. "Here we go. Tallahassee."

Toothy and tan, tall hi-lit hair. I said, "Smoothie boy's a nope."

~~~

Ranger Randy bedeviled Dwight by being scarce online. The man didn't even have a facebook page, which appeared to provoke and offend Dwight and confound his expectations.

I consoled him as best I could. "Might be dead," I told him.

Dwight kept at it, of course, and turned up a quartet of possibles in time. One of them was a statistics professor at James Madison, out in the valley. We set him aside and stayed on the other three. They all had records, petty stuff, drunk and disorderly, menacing.

"I'll find him," Dwight said. "Hey, ask a favor?"

"Shoot."

He wondered if I'd rough up his sister's boyfriend. Before I could finish squinting at him good, Dwight pointed at Gus and told me, "She said you might."

So I shifted around to Gus.

"We looked you up," she told me. "Sounds like you used to be kind of a shitbag."

I couldn't argue with her. "Put it behind me," I said.

"Did you?" Gus asked.

I nodded.

"So now you just hire people for it?"

"What are you on about?"

"Woman in the Best Buy lot. Who are you exactly?"

That was the moment they both appeared to want me to unpack my sordid past, reveal the path I'd traveled before we'd met, acquaint them with rocky experiences I'd known and life lessons I'd collected, the strange turns I'd taken that had lead me to driving a Suffolk loan shark around, but that was not my kind of thing at all.

"What did your sister's boyfriend do?" I asked Dwight.

"Something probably," Dwight said. "Or he will."

By that time, case 873946/B was doing in our command center pretty much what it had been up to for years in the Mathis' Chuckatuck car shed. I'd say two months passed when we'd get together and accomplish next to nothing at all, especially on the Randy Pyle front. He was proving unfindable, so we tackled another local job to give ourselves a break.

The battery went missing from Dwight's mother's Impala, and Dwight did his usual sort of creative hacking to finger the kids who'd boosted it, a pair from around the corner, juvenile versions of Carson and Miles — ambitious but low on decency and indifferent to people as a rule.

There was a burned-out house a couple of blocks over with a garden hut in the back yard. The owner was fighting with his insurer, so the property had been long neglected, which made that hut at the back of the lot an ideal stash for boosted stuff.

"I followed them," Dwight explained to me. "Not too bright."

There were six or eight batteries inside along with all manner of stuff people had left in their cars. Travel mugs. Coats. Book satchels and a few purses. Gym shoes. Elaborate ice scrapers and jugs of antifreeze, quarts of oil.

"Why bother?" I asked Dwight, the universe too a little.

"Bored probably. We get that way."

Then he took photos of everything and used them for some sort of social network shaming and skullduggery that landed those boys in trouble all over the place. I think they cut grass and raked leaves for six months steady. They cleaned out gutters, washed cars, stained a few decks, just about anything their neighbors decided needed doing. It didn't mean they wouldn't be Miles and Carson. They'd just not be them quite so soon.

Gus followed up with a distraction of her own, or rather a big Jeremy related item. He had a problem with a rival at his country club, a man in need of a beat down.

"He wants your girl, the one who punched him."

"Not sure that's her regular thing."

"He'll pay plenty."

"I'm doing him favors now?"

"Want to talk about it in the closet?"

I did. We did. Carla demanded triple her usual rate, but the country club guy turned out to be such a deserving ogre that Carla happily took double instead.

"He thinks we ought to get a drink or something," Gus announced to me right after.

"Me and you and Jeremy?"

"Dwight too."

"He's fifteen."

"Old fifteen, and he knows a stripper."

"I don't think I'm quite that civilized."

I didn't get the feeling Gus was either by the way she said, "All right."

Vilmer Demarest was due an update, so I went to Magnolia Hills to see him after staying away a handful of Thursdays. It was tougher than I'd expected to go back into that place with its rackets and its aromas, its memories for me of Homer which, truth be told, was probably more about my mother than him. A few of the attendants there looked at me sideways like maybe I'd forgotten

my resident geezer was dead, but I knew just
where I was going and found Vilmer in his usual
chair. He watched me come and even seemed to
place me, didn't bother with "Hey, listen" anyway.

Mr. Demarest was having a good afternoon.
Maybe the light was right or the temperature
favorable, the pressure in his cranium ideal. I
can't really say, but he was as tuned as I'd ever
found him. He didn't recite the file identifier or
get snagged by the fire alarm. He just watched
me come, watched me sit, and then greeted me
with, "So?"

I could do the quick, efficient thing, just hadn't
expected to need to. "Rode out to Simmons Gap,"
I told him. "Been there?"

He went glum and nodded.

"Lonely spot."

Another nod.

"You ever talk to the ranger?"

He strained but came up with it. "Pyle?"

I nodded now.

"Once."

"Get a feel for him?"

"Kind of off," he told me.

"Off how?"

Mr. Demarest picked out an acoustical ceiling
tile and paid full attention to it as he spoke.

"You'd think he'd say one thing, but he'd tell you something else."

I felt like I knew just what he meant. You assume people walk around with a shared frame of reference, common basic assumptions about how life on the planet should be conducted and how things probably ought to go, but then you run across a Randy Pyle who thinks something otherwise entirely, and he musters his world with the casual ease that you usually muster yours. You think he'll say one thing, but he tells you something else.

"Worth a conversation?"

Vilmer didn't say yes and didn't say no, didn't appear to have an opinion, but he did flash a yellow incisor as he told me, "You're no better off than me.

That's a cold case for you, the great equalizer. Half addled Sunoco man and lousy ex cop both brought low.

ii

I knew Dwight's mother a little, enough to make her comfortable with me, and it helped that she believed my house was full of gadgets I lacked the sense to operate and mend. She had a smart TV she couldn't turn on unless Dwight was there to help her, so if my network was down or my boot loader was balky or my PC and my printer were on the outs, then it seemed only reasonable that Dwight would spend his after-school hours at my house.

But then he broke with protocol and carried some forensic photos home. His mother found them in his book bag because that's how she kept up with him. She came straight over and brought Dwight with her, and she was waving the photos at me before I'd opened the door all the way.

Here name was Belia, and she was a Slovakian with a curious strain of English. Her sentences usually came out backwards, and she used words like 'dauncy' and 'chockers' that she'd gotten out of the books the previous owner had left in their house. He was before my time, but by the looks of his library and the tenacious stink of his pipe tobacco, I'd say he was a stay-at-home anglophile with holes in all his cardigans. Dwight's mom had done some powerful cleaning when she and Dwight and his sister moved in, but there was only so much devoted eccentric you could hope to exorcise.

"I'm very crumpsy, mister," Belia told me as she smacked me in the chest with the photos.

I was sorry to see Belia crumpsy. I far preferred her chuffed, and I'd come across her once dressed up for a date when she was 'on the pull', she told me. I'd had to look that one up and felt fairly certain she'd missed the thrust of the thing.

"What, mister?" She ordinarily called me mister, sometimes Jack, which wasn't actually my name.

"My fault," I told her. "Dwight's been helping me with a case."

"For dosh?"

"Sure, yeah. It's official and all."

Belia could just see into our command center from where she was standing. There were forensic photos on display, one particularly nasty picture of Abigail Tucker's face. Some taut skin. Quite a few exposed teeth.

"Oh, mister." Belia left us and charged in for a closer look.

"Jesus," I said to Dwight.

He did that shame thing boys of his age do and dogs of any vintage. He dropped his head and rolled his eyes up at me.

"Mister."

I pushed Dwight ahead of me into the spare room. Belia was soaking in the photos and various forensic documents on display, and the stuff she was seeing was hitting her pretty hard.

She pointed at a weathered chunk of Abigail Tucker's torso.

"She went missing a few years ago. We're trying to figure out why."

Dwight tapped his chest and told his mother, "Technical consultant."

She didn't seem terribly impressed. Then she noticed a photo I'd taken, printed, and posted on the board. Gus from the rear, studying the evidence. As was customary with Gus, she'd left her jeans on the sofa and was wearing just a paisley blouse and a pair of sky blue panties.

Dwight could have backed me up on that one but instead just said, "Uh oh."

I calmed Belia down, and we worked it out, and I took a call in the middle of the whole thing from Benny about a problem at his gentleman's club. Miles and Carson (they way their sort will) had decided to spit the bit. They'd rehired their chef buddy and printed up an hors d'oeuvres menu

which strayed considerably from chicken wings
and popcorn shrimp. There was some kind of
Catalan sausage on it in romesco sauce,
bruschetta four ways, and Chesapeake oysters
with green apple mignonette.

Worse still, they'd hired two girls they'd known
from college in Charlottesville — Mindy and Carol
who couldn't between them pretend that our
patrons weren't skeevy. Some whiskery guy who
smelled like a culvert would give one or the other
of them a wrecked dollar bill just to buy fifteen
seconds of his nose in their cleavage or something
of the sort. For his trouble, he'd get an "As if!"
face, maybe even a smack or a shove, and he'd
look around bewildered wondering how he'd paid
for that.

I tried to talk to Miles and Carson, but their
bruises and cuts had healed, so they'd allowed
themselves to all but forget what Benny had told
them and how. I could have thrashed them a bit
myself, but that wasn't really my thing. Or rather
it was so completely Benny's thing that I felt like I
ought to leave him to it.

I used to carry a sap. The first cop I worked
with gave it to me. Some oldster had passed the
thing to him. It was a hunk of lead in palm-oiled
leather with a rat tail you held it by to generate
momentum, and that thing would put the biggest,

dumbest lowlife right to sleep. Primitive I know but marginally creative given that now most cops just pull out their side arms and blast away. Carson and Miles were perfect candidates for a sapping. You didn't want to kill them, but you wanted them stunned and hurt, left in a couple of drooling piles.

But I'd lost my itch to crack heads and was content to let Benny do all the thumping those boys rated and deserved. They were smug and insulting and not very bright but confident of their splendor, which I could recognize and object to and yet still leave them both untouched. It may sound like a little thing, but it struck me as a significant personal evolution. It's a lot of work to be angry and violent, and I hoped that in my golden years I could lead a more measured and placid sort of life. There was an irate guy with a dogwood staff on the way over from Emporia, and I was content to wait for him to arrive.

Benny was in a dire state by the time he came into the club. He was fed up with Carson and Miles and ready to find an outlet for some pent up aggravation. It didn't help that Miles and Carson had bought a big Victorian mirror that they'd hung behind the bar and written the hors d'oeuvre menu on. The thing just served as further incitement for Benny who didn't as a rule draw pleasure from thumping people twice because the second time around spoke poorly of his powers of persuasion.

So there was sadness to Benny blended in with the pitch of rage that Carson and Miles had a gift for bringing out. Benny adjusted his grip on his dogwood staff and said to them both, "All right," which they pretended they couldn't quite understand, what with the extra spit and all.

It turned out those brothers had recruited a couple of beefy guys to help protect them, two bouncers who came in from outside once Benny had started in with the whacking. I didn't recognize them — muscle freaks with an unfortunate ratio of bicep to brain. I looked for the stoutest chair I could find and ended up with a barstool, but I didn't even have to use it since cousin Dennis rose to the occasion. He wasn't much of a driver for Benny — had a miserable sense of direction —but he proved himself as fierce and loyal as blood kin probably comes.

Dennis went after those boys with anything he could lay his hands on — bottles, chairs, a napkin dispenser and, finally, a fire extinguisher. I would have helped him, but Dennis was far too frantic to get near. He lashed out at anything that wandered within reach, which was those two bouncers chiefly, but he did catch a patron on the elbow. Luckily the guy was too drunk to care.

Carson and Miles, with no help coming, weren't up to fending off Benny themselves and soon suffered the brand of injuries I'd seen plenty of before. Fractures, bruises, parted skin. Those boys begged Benny to stop, and he even did after a while but primarily to have a word with Dennis.

"Might leave it at that," Benny told his cousin just as Dennis was about to commit manslaughter. Then Benny pointed at Dennis and said to me, "New boss here. What do you think?"

And that's how I got altogether out of the strip club business and back under the wheel of Benny's New Yorker part-time, which proved a fine arrangement for everybody, possibly excepting Dwight until he saw Tammy in the CVS without her stripper duds and her face paint and decided pep squad girls would suit him fine.

~~~~

Cousin Dennis proved to be a perfect fit with the girls and the clientele since he was tough and hopelessly sleazy and ate any damn thing that came to hand. He filled the club up by catering to himself while Miles and Carson slinked off to Montauk to recover.

I guess Benny had decided I'd paved a righteous path for Dennis, and he returned the favor by directing me to the Kennards one afternoon. Life was good for Benny at that moment. People were meeting their obligations, and he'd taken an interest in a woman who treated him like he was normal. Mags, he called her. She claimed to have a brother with CP who couldn't walk or talk, could barely swallow, which made her sympathetic (she said).

There was something about her that sat poorly with me. I noticed she kind of shut down when she was out of Benny's view. She'd go slack like she was relaxing, off the stage for a moment. Mags happened to be with us that day in Chuckatuck when the Kennards had us in.

Their house wasn't much. Tidy but small and on a piece of sandy property with a yard that was primarily mulch. Spindly trees. Scraggly bushes. Busted whelk shells tossed around for that nautical, bayside look, even though we were a good half hour from the water.

He was Hal. She was Shelly. I don't know exactly what Benny told them, but they'd set up for us in their dining room with cookies and hot tea and lots of Abigail Tucker memorabilia, most of it in a couple of ring binders. We started with refreshments and chat before Benny and Mags retired to the back deck so I could explain to the Kennards what I was up to, who I was up to it for, and why.

"Why you?" Shelly Kennard quite justifiably wanted to know.

"Used to be a cop." I gave them enough biography to put them both at ease. "Told Mr. Demarest I'd have a sniff around for him. Hope that's ok."

They guessed it was.

"Got a few questions."

They might have been through this ad nauseam but not lately, so they proved eager enough.

"You thought Abigail was in her bedroom?"

They both nodded.

"She had a boyfriend, right?"

They named him. Halfback playing away.

"Police think she snuck out. How about you?"

They nodded again.

"Had she done it before?"

They consulted with a look. Another nod.

"To see who? Go where?"

More silent consultation.

"Won't go past this room," I told them.

"Abby had a . . . friend," Hal said.

"Not from school," Shelly added. "Looked older."

That snagged my attention. "Police hear about him?" There was no reference to this person in the file.

Hal nodded. Shelly chimed in. "We only saw him once. In the road. I woke up."

"Definitely not the half back?"

They nodded. Consulted again. "Then we found something," Shelly said as Hal got up off the sofa and left the room. I heard him open a drawer in the kitchen. He came back in with a plain white business envelope and handed the thing to me.

"It was in her closet." Shelly again. "I was cleaning out one day, what . . . ?She turned towards Hal. ". . . three years after?"

He nodded.

I lifted the envelope flap to find a solitary Polaroid and pulled it out. It was photo of Abigail Tucker from about the collarbones up. Bare shoulders. Flush skin. She was wearing a ball gag, the kind with the full head harness. Lots of leather and hardware, buckles and rivets. The ball was yellow and had air holes in it. Her lips around it were moist and pink. Her hazel eyes were on the lens, and she didn't look to be in distress.

There was a hand in the photo, a man's hand, laid out flat across her breastbone. Thumb up. Fingers extended. Only the first two were in the frame. Veiny, muscular, a bit on the grimy side. The sort of hand you'd be happy enough to see holding your plug wires or your dip stick but not touching your teenaged daughter's naked flesh.

I flipped the photo over just in case there was a helpful scrawl on the back, the name of the man and his phone number maybe, his parole officer's address.

"Police seen this?"

The Kennards shook their heads. Hal explained they'd discussed turning the snapshot in but had decided it would only serve to sully their Abby's reputation. I knew just what they were getting at because I'd seen plenty of it before. People as a general rule want homicide victims to have it coming since that makes it all more tolerable and, as carnage goes, ok. So if she'd gotten herself in with a bad sort and had done some questionable things, then Abigail dead could seem a lot less senseless and random.

"Her friends from school know about him?"

"Said not," Shelly told me, sounding considerably short of convinced.

"I've got two names in the file but no statements, just notes. Once of them's . . . Marie?"

"Maria," Shelly said. "And CeCe."

"They still around?"

They both nodded.

"Think maybe I could have a look at Abigail's stuff?"

They were quick to allow it, didn't hesitate at all. Hal led me down the hallway and pointed me into Abigail's bedroom, which wasn't one of those shrines like you see sometimes but just a mix of leftover girly possessions along with their own. An ironing board, a laundry hamper, and a twin bed that was stacked neatly with towels and linen. The clothes hanging in the closet looked chiefly to be Hal's. The shoes on the shelf and floor were his as well.

There was a small desk with empty drawers. Abigail was confined mostly to the wall shelves. Snapshots of her. A journal with only three pages filled. A New Testament watercolor of Jesus healing a batch of unfortunates. There was stuff of hers on a corkboard as well. The thing was shingled with magazine pages, hand-drawn doodles, colored notecards written over in loopy, girlish script.

The Kennards let me keep the Polaroid. I think they just wanted it out of the house, so I thanked them and took it with me. Benny had a word with Hal and Shelly on the front walk while I went on to the car and waited there with Mags, the two of us together leaning against the fender.

"Sweet man, isn't he?" she said as we watched Benny hug Shelly Kennard and then take Hal's hand in both of his own.

That was hardly the word I would have used. "Can be," I allowed.

iii

I stuck the Polaroid up on our corkboard along with the addresses of Abigail's girlfriends, and I asked Dwight to cyber stalk them, which appeared to be his calling and his gift.

He'd never seen a ball gag. "What's that for?" he asked.

"Sex thing."

That only clouded the issue since sex for Dwight, at that point, took place exclusively in his lap, which meant he couldn't begin to understand how a whiffle ball might help.

Gus came in a quarter hour later, and I told Dwight, "Ask her."

Gus joined us in the command center carrying what looked like a freighted duffel, which she dropped on the floor as she pulled off her oversized shades.

Her left eye socket was bruised and puffy. They eyeball itself was inflamed and red. "Hey, bunky," was all she said.

Dwight was a wise enough kid to know when it was better to be scarce. Normal people would probably have embraced. Gus would have sobbed, and I would have sputtered, but we were both too down on humanity for that. Past the shock and the rage and well into the resignation. I didn't even ask for an explanation. She'd said or done something that got her a smack. The details hardly mattered.

Gus had seen a doctor. He'd given her drops and established that no bones were fractured. I had a bag of broccoli in the freezer that helped to keep the swelling down. She wasn't hungry, so we had no dinner beyond a half bottle of rye. I only asked her one punch-related question.

"About me?"

"About me," she said.

I studied her bruise and remembered. I must have Sicilian in me somewhere because I'm damn fine at vengeance eventually and in time.

I lived in a walkup in Brooklyn once with a deplorable downstairs neighbor whose wife had died, leaving him and his daughter on the parlor floor. The girl was fifteen when I moved in, and her dad used to knock her around. I could hear them and saw the evidence, but I didn't horn in straightaway since I knew she'd be the one to suffer for it.

When she turned eighteen, she left for college in Pennsylvania, and I went downstairs and knocked on the door.

Dad answered — Sameer, from Yemen. We knew each other a bit in that meaningless, neighborly way like you do. Hellos in passing on the front stoop, nods at the garbage bin.

"Been keeping something for you," I told him.

He looked confused but a bit delighted. Then I punched him hard in the kidney and helped him sit in a big pleather chair. I worked him over, all neck-down stuff, did it slowly and with precision. He threatened to have me arrested, so I showed him my shield and punched him some more.

Like I said, I was not a good cop, but I was effective in my way. I was a big believer back then in balance, how everything was an offset, and you could stand to be despicable if you made up for it over time.

Gus took some aspirin and went to bed. I spent the night on the sofa thinking about a dead girl with a yellow ball gag and a live woman with a bloody eye.

I woke up to find Gus at my kitchen dinette studying the Polaroid. It was barely light out, but some jackass neighbor already had his leaf blower going.

She waved the snapshot at me.

"Talked to her parents . . . the Kennards," I told her. "Said they found that a couple of years after."

"And the guy?"

"Not Johnny halfback. And Dwight wants 411 on the head gear."

"Looks . . . unhelpful."

"That's kind of where he is."

"I don't do hardware."

"Closet rods."

"Found art," was what she said.

It was Thursday, and Benny had cut me loose, had an outing cooked up with Mags, so I persuaded Gus to ride with me out to Magnolia Hills, did it mostly by promising her lunch. We were there by ten and found Vilmer Demarest in his usual spot. He had on a tidy gingham dress shirt and pants that quit well below his pectorals, so by institutional standards, he was a regular fashion plate. The hair hanging from his nostrils even appeared to be laying one way.

I had to tap him to get him off the shiny, red alarm box. I introduced Gus who removed her shades as she met him, and her bruised face appeared to register with Vilmer and prick him because decent people never wither and age out of decency. Gus' eye took over as the thing he studied instead of the fire alarm.

I told Mr. Demarest about the Kennards. He appeared to be listening to me. I had Gus show him the Polaroid. He took it from her and had a study.

"Ever get wind of a boyfriend on the side?" I asked him.

He seemed to go a little teary. The sight of Abigail Tucker with that ball in her mouth? Or maybe the hand near her throat? I couldn't tell, but it sure wasn't just rheumy eyes from being ninety-something.

"How about her girlfriends? You talk to them?" His scant notes suggested he might have.

Mr. Demarest nodded. He considered Gus' puffy eye socket. "Colby," he told her.

"Norfolk cop," I reminded her. "Junior guy on the case."

"Is he on the ball?" she asked him.

That's when the fire alarm took hold, and we lost Vilmer Demarest to the far wall.

I tried to cash in my lunch promise at the diner up the road, but we were barely in the lot before Gus informed me, "Uh uh."

She didn't want something better necessarily, just expensive and pretentious. "A proper hostess," she said. "A real waiter. Maybe a guy with a basket of rolls."

"Is that French place still downtown?"

It was, and she knew just how to get there.

Benny would have loved it since the food came pre-mashed. The chef was deep into plate decoration with smudges and smears and dollops of stuff, nothing too big to be troublesome or even remotely filling. We had authentic Chablis and Sevre et Belle butter, some caramel thing for desert that looked to have been singed with a torch.

Gus got plenty of stares from the clientele — mostly local Norfolk attorneys and ladies who were as wiry as refugees. I got some sidelong attention myself.

"They think I hit you," I said.

"And now you're buying me off. Why in the world wouldn't they think it?"

One of the women actually waved at Gus. "Friend of yours?"

She waved back. "Jeremy's mother."

The lady got up from her table and started over to us.

"You're my lawyer," Gus told me, and that's how she presented me to Barbara who gave me precisely the sneering notice a daughter-in-law's attorney should get.

Barbara didn't appear to take any notice of Gus' injury. She mentioned a party she was planning, some sort of birthday event at her club, and she wanted Gus to save the date in case Jeremy forgot. That was it really. Gus got a "Ta ta". I didn't rate so much as a glance. Gus waited until Barbara was back in her chair before she climbed onto my lap and made a showy spectacle of sticking her tongue in my ear.

Barbara glanced our way and could have seen us if she cared to, but I felt sure she'd gone to selective blue-blood focus, which lets unpleasant things be fuzzy and so, essentially, not there.

Gus couldn't cook, or maybe just wouldn't, so I drove Benny when he needed me, planned our meals, and did the bulk of the grocery shopping while Gus and Dwight worked the case. That chiefly involved them conjuring theories based on the evidence at hand when Gus wasn't explaining females to Dwight and fielding his pep squad questions. I'd make supper for the three of us those nights when Dwight's mom was on the pull.

So we were sort of a family organized around a homicide. Instead of blood and genetics to bind us, we had a dead girl in the woods. And not even recently dead or someone we'd known, which made it all that much stranger, but that didn't keep us from being effective, or keep Dwight from being it anyway. He located the high school girlfriends, their resumes, their facebook pages, a few indecent Snapchat photos.

Gus gave those girls a story about the TV piece we were scouting and the very real chance they'd feature in a cable segment devoted to their murdered friend. That proved more than enough to land us a meeting with them at a Starbucks in Hampton, and it turned out those two were still chummy in a cocktails-twice-a-year sort of way.

They were catching up at an outside table when Gus and I arrived. Maria worked as a dental technician and was wearing a pair of teal scrubs while CeCe had kind of a Junior League thing going — pastel pantsuit and treacly insincerity.

Gus was ballsy and efficient and made enough sense to Maria and CeCe to tempt them to tell us whatever we needed to know. That's where I came in since I was the producer with the notebook who'd jotted down a half dozen areas of interest to pursue.

I started soft the way you like too, got their general accounts which let them compete some twelve years later for Abigail Tucker's special affection — who was her primo confidant and her bestest friend. They had a scrum about that, and once it grew a little starchy, I moved on to the boyfriend. Tim the halfback.

"Ought to see him now," Maria said and snorted. "Sure got a way with a fork."

"He live around here?"

They both nodded. "Sells tractors or something," CeCe told me. She pointed vaguely north.

"How about the other boyfriend?" I pulled out the Polaroid and flashed it at them. They both seemed insufficiently surprised, but still had nothing to say.

"Whole story or no story," Gus told them.

"What do you want to know?" CeCe asked us.

"He got a name?"

"Mister," Maria told me. "That's what we called him."

"We only saw him," CeCe started in a looked Maria's way, " . . . once?"

Maria nodded.

"Where?"

"Buckroe."

I knew it, a beach not five miles from where we were.

"I think that's where she met him," CeCe said.

"He was old, you know?" Maria said. "Like twenty-five, maybe thirty."

"How did she end up with him?" Gus asked. "What was the charm?"

"He was pretty good looking. Might have had money." Marie pointed at the Polaroid. "And Abby was kind of wild."

Then they started asking about our shooting schedule and quizzing Gus chiefly on budgets and appearance fees and the like. Gus clearly had the fabulist's touch and did some breezy, persuasive lying. By the time she finished, I was half convinced we'd be back for filming in three months.

"What do you think?" Gus asked me as we watched Maria and CeCe dodge the Starbucks drive-thru traffic and climb into their cars.

"Get Dwight on the guy, I guess."

"Buckroe?" she asked.

We went across on Pembroke and left the car in the park there by the shore. Buckroe beach is wide and sandy. Lots of access. Blue collar mostly. It's got a pier to the south and an inlet to the north and faces east onto the Chesapeake with a view of the bridge/tunnel in the distance.

Gray day, and the wind had some bite off the water, so there was just a handful of hardy souls walking the shore.

"Summertime you could sure meet all sorts of people here."

"She said he had money."

I reminded, "She also said he was old. You know, twenty-five."

We walked that beach from end to end.

"It's like this, isn't it?" Gus asked after a quarter hour of silence.

"What?"

"Policing. You do a lot of going where people were."

She was right, of course, even if I hadn't ever
thought about it in quite that way. Warm case or
cold case, you were hardly ever on time. You
started late and just grew more tardy, so while
that first-twenty-four-hours thing about
homicides might be true, it could just as well be
the first quarter hour or the initial seven minutes.
You only show up after, and from there you drop
off the pace.

"Yeah," I told Gus, looking out over the water.
"I've been a lot of places like this doing exactly
what we're doing."

"Does it ever help?"

"Sometimes. You get your landmarks down,
run across reluctant civilians, but with a case this
old, we're just walking on the beach."

"You don't think we ought to quit, do you?"

I shook my head. "Promised Vilmer."

"He'll never know."

"I will."

~ ~ ~

Benny, of all people, had an in with detective
Colby, Lawrence Colby who wouldn't stand for
'Larry'.

We were heading up to Portsmouth when
Benny asked me about the case. Just me and him.
He'd kind of gone off Mags. I hadn't seen her in a

week and a half by then and had asked him about her, just being polite.

Benny winked, I remember, and told me, "She'll be fine."

"Found your killer yet?" he asked me. He was reading the WSJ editorial page at the time, which regularly featured the variety of white, puckered lunacy sure to put Benny in a lively mood.

I found him in the mirror and shook my head. "Need a word with a guy. A cop."

"Local?"

"Norfolk. Colby."

Benny chuckled and eyed his paper. "Tomorrow good?"

It was. Benny put us together in a park just off the beltway. Eight in the morning with the traffic stacked up and Detective Lawrence Colby in a decidedly pissy mood. There was a swing set and a roundabout, a couple of half-dilapidated picnic tables. A public toilet that was locked shut and a water fountain that didn't work.

"So?" he asked me before I'd even arrived where he was standing.

I'd been relieved of the obligation to treat the man with gratitude since a guy who owed Benny favor had nothing special coming.

"Abigail Tucker."

A deep breath. A slight nod.

"Interested in the boyfriend."

He squinted. "You mean the kid from . . .?

I shook my head. I pulled the Polaroid out of my jacket pocket and held it up. "Him."

"Where'd you get that?" I let him take the photo from me and give it a full once-over.

"Kennards. They found it squirreled away."

"He got a name?"

I shrugged. "I'm told she met him at Buckroe. Late twenties, maybe thirty. With money. Anybody in your file like that?"

He shook his head and handed the photo back.

"But you'll look for me, right? Benny thinks you ought to."

"I needed a bump," Colby told me, "and I paid him back. No shame in that."

"Fine," I said. "Then you can do it for the right reasons."

We both stalked off to our shitty sedans like matadors or something. Another bit of business tainted by testosterone.

I had to hustle back home to work my shift with Benny. Marco was out of his latest stint in the lockup and so, by rights, should have been driving instead, but he'd celebrated a bit too vigorously and had gotten into a dust-up. Three dust-ups if you're counting and all of them during his first night loose.

"Rum," Benny had explained to me. We both knew about rum and Marco and were aware that once he'd gone over his dosage there was a lot that could go wrong. Fortunately, he wasn't back inside for aggravated assault and felony mischief because Benny had seen to it Marco flew home to Santo Domingo. "Be six weeks," Benny said. He'd done the math and knew who he had to pay off and how.

So I had steady work for another stretch with Benny, which was thinking time for me while Gus and Dwight got up to whatever they pleased at the command center back home. They did some snooping and theorizing, but there was plenty of fooling around on the internet and female advice for Dwight as well.

A couple of days after Colby, Benny directed me to a house due south of Suffolk hard by the Dismal Swamp. All farmland and bear scat and twelve-pack boxes. The place where we stopped was backed right onto the marsh. There was a truck in the yard, an old Henrico County ambulance that had been thinly painted over (by the looks of it) with a roller.

I waited for instructions, but Benny didn't give any. We sat. The engine idled. I finally found him in the mirror.

"Give it a toot," he said, and I was reaching for the horn when the front door of the house swung open. "Hold it."

Mags came out. She got ushered out really. I saw a man's arm up to the elbow as he guided her onto the front landing. Pressed white shirt, buttoned to the wrist. Then the door closed behind her. She looked back at it. She turned our way but stayed right where she was.

"Go on," Benny told me, so I gave the horn a couple of toots, and Mags eased into the yard, moving slowly. She carried herself like a woman who'd just had several organs removed.

I reached for my door handle, intended to get out and help her, but Benny told me, "Stay put," so that's exactly what I did.

He let her open the back door for herself and patted the seat to bid her climb in. She did it without a word and without a look at either of us.

She wasn't injured anywhere that I could see, but the Mags who'd climbed into the Chrysler was hardly the woman who'd raised my suspicions, the woman who'd given off deviousness like a scent. That Mags was gone. The one we picked up swampside was a changed creature, a defeated, muted thing.

On the way back north, Benny read his paper and had me start Alcina in act two. Mags, for her part, stared out the side window, and I saw her flinch ever so slightly when Benny reached to touch her hand.

I was a troubled man at quitting time because of that broken woman, and I arrived home primed to lay it out and get a read from Gus, but she and Dwight met me at the front door, the pair of them little short of giddy.

"There's another one," Gus told me.

"Another what?"

"Show him."

Dwight had his phone in hand and turned the screen for me to see it. There was text on it I couldn't begin to make out, a photo I couldn't quite see.

"What is it?"

"Julie Fay Greer," Dwight said. "Fifteen. Spotsylvania County."

"Missing four years." Gus took a turn. "They found her last week in the woods."

"And get this," Dwight told me. "She was wearing a daisy ring."

BullittBoy27

i

We drove out to the Spotsylvania woods. They insisted, but it seemed mostly ghoulish to me and not likely to produce anything beyond a tasteless thrill.

"Who went to Simmons Gap?" Gus asked me, so I shut right on up.

The tape was still up here and there, bright yellow against the gray oak trunks and the brown leaf litter. You could see where they'd set up a tent and scraped the forest debris away.

"Found her here probably," Dwight told us and poked a depression with the toe of his sneaker.

Him and Gus were percolating with possibilities and theories, and I left them to rattle around and chatter while I found a rock to park on. It wasn't a tough spot to get to. We had a black top maybe a quarter mile east and a gravel road a little closer to the north. I could see Gus' Volvo from where I sat, so the dumping would have been far less of a chore for this one than Abigail Tucker.

"She interfered with?" Gus asked me.

They were picking up the lingo. "Don't know. Paper's only got her name and age so far."

"But strangled, right?" Dwight this time.

I nodded. "According to your internet guy."

Dwight had found a homicide freak on the web who seemed even keener on killings than they were. He came off as a supremely confident amateur who'd be out in the world putting thorny murder cases to rest if he didn't have comment threads to fill or could be bothered to put on pants.

He went by BullittBoy27 and seemed to specialize in sneering. His site was frantic with blinking advertisements (for hair growth ointments, reverse mortgages, diet pills, sex aids), and to hear it from him, the cops usually had the wrong end of everything. They couldn't string clues together or decipher forensics the way he could. Usually, BullittBoy27 held off naming culprits for 'judicial reasons', but rare was the crime he hadn't buttoned up and figured out.

I'd developed a fair sense of BullittBoy27 merely from reading his blog. "Probably works at a Hardee's," I said, "scared of girls. I could be wrong, though. He might just be twelve."

Dwight objected with a snort and informed us he'd located BullittBoy27, and it turned out he was well within our reach. The bill for his internet service went to a post office box on Chincoteague Island, so he was only a leisurely drive up the eastern shore.

"He knows stuff," Dwight assured us as he poked glumly at the packed earth with a stick.

There was nothing to see in that forest beyond stomped ground and police leavings. Little to imbibe but woodland desolation. I might have felt worse about being there — the day-trip voyeurism of it — but for the gloom that took hold of Dwight and Gus, which was useful and instructive.

Back when I was in uniform, I'd lurk at the edges of stuff. You'd show up at a murder, and your job was to keep civilians away from the gore. They'd hang sheets or put up canopies, do what they could to frustrate the gawking, but the easiest way to manage it was to shove everybody back. People objected and quarreled with us. They were legitimately fascinated and often insisted they had an American claim to know exactly what had happened and to whom. They didn't realize how lucky they were that we let them see so little.

Once you stand over a murder victim, the waste of it hits you hard. The squandered purpose. The frantic magic of life itself snuffed out. You can't avoid the feeling it leaves you with — of loss and aching sadness. It always finds you, found me sitting on my rock in the Spotsylvania woods, and that dead girl was two weeks in the morgue by then. It hit Gus and Dwight as well. I pretty much saw it happen. They were considering the dent in the ground where the body had lain, and the grim futility of it all just crept up and chilled them deep.

Gus made a noise, an involuntary moan, and Dwight had a look around, keen for somewhere else to be.

"Let's go," Gus said with some urgency.

"Yeah." Dwight was right there with her, and they'd both hustled off to Gus' Volvo before I'd gotten off my rock.

We stopped at a Mickey D's on the way home, and I had one of those tepid milkshakes that's all chemistry and sugar while Dwight shared with me and Gus some BullittBoy27 info.

"Something's wrong with him."

A high hanger, but I let it pass.

"I mean like wheelchair wrong," Dwight said and then acquainted us with the last six months of BullittBoy's medicare records.

That helped explain the tone of his prose. He had bitter and impatient for a baseline and incandescent within easy reach.

"What's his real name?" I asked.

Dwight wouldn't tell me, so Gus did.

"Everett Parker Flynn."

"BullittBoy," Dwight insisted. "Wheelchair's bad enough."

"Drive up?" Gus asked.

I was prepared at that moment to go as far as, "Maybe."

I had the time in the week to do it because Marco had returned from Boca Chica and was back behind the wheel of Benny's Chrysler, and I was happy to be on limited service since I was feeling conflicted about Benny. More conflicted anyway. He was a loan shark after all who laid people's scalps open with a stick.

Mags is what bothered me. She was a wholly different creature after her interlude by the swamp. Not so much docile as shattered. No pluck. No will. No deviousness for sure. I knew people didn't get that way through the power of suggestion, which left me wondering exactly what Benny had put the woman through.

I didn't see terribly much of Mags, only enough to haunt and plague me. On one Saturday in particular she rode with us all day but barely did any talking. She looked out the window. She held Benny's hand. She'd wander when Benny took a client meeting. She mashed up his burger at lunch and fed it to him dutifully, but I didn't get the feeling her demeanor would change much if Benny had choked and fallen out.

That Dismal Swamp house where we'd picked her up turned out to be a rental, and Dwight tracked down the lease agreement for me. The lady who'd signed it was doing time in Ohio for bank fraud, and the rent payer of record for the current quarter was a man named Jerome Knighten. He had a Pearisburg address that was printed on his checks, a town down around Roanoke that's a stone's throw from West Virginia.

Dwight did some digging. Jerome Knighten had been a tank gunner, wounded in November of '44. His government checks were still getting cashed, but the utility had cut off his Pearisburg power for nonpayment. This was all stuff Dwight needed maybe twenty minutes to find.

"Might have moved up here," Gus suggested.

I wasn't feeling optimistic. "Give me the address," I told Dwight.

I called the Pearisburg volunteer fire department and reported a residential blaze. Those boys found Jerome Knighted wrapped up in a bedspread in his basement. He was laid out on a ping pong table, probably six months deceased.

"He's got a granddaughter," Dwight told me. "Sally Knighten." He showed me her booking shot on his screen. "Theft," he said, "Solicitation. Two breaking and entering charges. Picked up with this guy."

Dwight shifted to a mugshot of a gentleman named Diego. Guatemalan national with a brother named Juan who'd done federal time for distribution. I scanned Diego's charge sheet — unlawful restraint, menacing, two counts of sodomy.

"What's that mean?" Dwight asked.

"Catch all," I said. "What state?"

"Georgia."

"Whatever they've decided is an unnatural sexual act. Could be romancing a goat, could be pep squad stuff."

It was the unlawful restraint charge that brought up a sour memory for me. I'd been detailed to a task force, which involved me and a dead-ender named Jerry sitting in a dark and empty apartment watching a woman across the street. The feds were on her for supplying counterfeit documents to Russian bagmen, mostly phony import tariff stuff but the occasional visa and passport too. Our job was to make a record of everybody who came and went, so we took photos and broke a lot of moo shu wind.

I was wandering and stretching one night on a break from the tedium when I saw a woman out our bathroom window. In fact, I heard her before I saw her. She was pleading and weeping and moaning. That window gave onto an air shaft, and she was across it and one floor down. You come across stuff like that in the city sometimes what with people all jammed up together, so I didn't think too much of it until I saw her get punched as well.

She was sitting on the floor in a kitchen, her back against the refrigerator. I could see the top of her head and her bare lower legs. Her ankles were bound with rope. Somebody grabbed a fistful of that woman's hair and shook her while I watched. She got a couple of slaps. She wept some more. It seemed worth looking into.

I called Jerry in. He was crowding retirement and half full of Irish whiskey. I had him look at the girl through the window. She was just sitting and sniffling by then.

"She's tied up," I said. "Getting smacked around."

"Want me to go with you?"

He was fishing for a "No".

I knocked on three wrong doors before I found the right one. A woman answered, a little woman in an apron. She turned out to be Filipino, and she spoke front-of-house restaurant English. She could point you to a table and give you proper change, but it was all Tagalog after that.

I could see just enough of the kitchen floor — across the front room and off an alcove — to cause me to push on in, and that lady set up a terrible fuss. She tried to run me through with a bike spoke. She had a vase full of the things, all sharpened and ready to go, and she was angling for a gap in my ribs when I swung on her hard and knocked her down.

The girl in the kitchen was Chinese, and she was tied to a water pipe. She didn't speak any English at all and looked dehydrated and about half starved, all drawn and sunken and filthy. There was a Thai girl in one of the bedrooms in about the same condition, and a boy who turned out to be eleven. He was in the cluttered bedroom closet.

I'd drawn my Ruger, kept expecting a man to show up any moment. I knew how men thought. I knew what men did. I knew how debased some men were, so I'd decided instinctively there had to be one or two behind this mess. The boy from the closet knew a little English, and I tried to get some answers from him. He turned out to be Malaysian, from some village up in the hills, and could talk his way into a dishwashing job or maybe onto a bus.

Once he saw that Filipino woman sprawled on the floor in the front room, the kid went wild and had nearly kicked her to pieces before I could pull him off.

It was only her, the way it turned out. There was no man involved at all, so I was obliged to relax a bit on my scope of degradation and invite in women as a group and class.

When that Filipino lady woke up, she'd say nothing but the name of her attorney. "Victor Klausman." If I heard it once, I heard it thirty times. Occasionally, for variety's sake, she'd add behind it, "Jew." It's hard to know where you'll find your monsters.

We took a vote on what to do about Jerome Knighten paying rent. It was unanimous — we liked a mystery — so we rode out to the Dismal Swamp in Gus' Volvo wagon. The plan was to find the house where I'd fetched Mags and then work out the details there, which is not in any useful sense a plan. It seemed likely I'd end up knocking on a door and asking impertinent questions, maybe to a pair of lowlife Guatemalan brothers who had a history of Georgia sodomy, whatever that might be.

It was a regular house, and I had no trouble finding it again, given the Henrico County ambulance in the yard. Trashy, yes, but no worse than most of the places out that way, which were all doomed to rot and sink in time due to the ongoing creep of the marshland. If the thickety vines and cypress saplings didn't take you over, then the bog was sure to undercut and sink you in the end. Property was cheap out there by the swamp. Nothing nailed together was lasting.

Gus parked up the road, and we watched the house.

"So?" Gus said. She and Dwight both looked at me.

"Guess I'll think of something." I opened my door and got out.

They didn't look worried. Dwight especially. Of course, of the three of us, he was the one who'd never been properly punched.

Naturally, that swampside house had a dog, a filthy mongrel living under a pile of pallets. He barked at me and came charging out, but he wasn't vicious just excitable.

He knew better than to follow me onto the porch. I knocked. Nothing. I glanced towards my team up the road and knocked again. I heard the framing creak and waited, had already decided what to say, and started with, "Hey, sorry for the bother," before the door had swung fully open.

A stink swept out, must and squalor, animal reek like a bear den. It was dark inside. They'd hung blankets on the windows. The man answering the door looked maybe forty, and he was wiry and dressed like a Mormon — white shirt, black trousers, sensible shiny shoes. He had a boy's regular haircut and acetone eyeglasses from, like, 1948.

"We got transformer trouble." I pointed nowhere much. "I'm checking your meter and need a look at your panel box. That okay?"

I smiled and waited. He eyeballed me good.

"It's back there." He pointed over his shoulder and stepped aside so I could come in.

The Knighten girl was in there, looked to be in a stupor on the sofa.

"How y'all?" I said to her.

She just squinted at me.

The guy pointed along a gloomy back hallway. "Down at the end, on the right."

The panel box was behind a fussy Victorian cabinet full of figurines and sheet music. The fuses were the old-timey screw in kind. I took one out and put it back, knocked around for a couple of minutes and then headed back up the hall.

The TV was playing in the front room, tuned to a chat show where a woman was cooking what she called a pilaf, but she added to it M&Ms and cheese. The man wasn't watching. Sally Knighten wasn't either. She was glassy-eyed on the sofa. The guy was in a straight-back table chair reading a fat book. The Portable Hobbes.

"Can't do much back there. That fuse box is out of code."

He sniffed, but it wasn't responsive. Just something he'd do anyway.

"Y'all might lose power off and on for the next little bit. Swapping out equipment down the line."

That earned me a nod. I told Sally Knighten, "M'am." I offered my hand to the guy, said, "I'm Tony."

"Leonard," he told me without bothering to shake. I saw myself out the door.

It was the better part of a half-mile up the road to Gus' Volvo, so I had time to think through all the details in my head. Leonard was just the sort of guy Benny would have in his sphere, tight-lipped but probably with a serious kink. Leonard would need money for various depravities, probably including bulk narcotics. Benny would float him for a quick return and accumulate chits with Leonard that he could call in.

It seemed likely that Mags had been working some kind of angle on Benny, and there I'd been worried that he was too smitten to notice. What didn't Benny notice? What had I ever known him to miss? Whatever he'd done, it had certainly taken. That much I felt sure of. Mags had come out of that house a creature who'd never work an angle again.

"Who's in there?" Dwight asked me once I'd finally reached the car.

"That Knighten girl, for one. Some guy named Leonard. I thought maybe I heard other people around but didn't see anybody."

I'd opened my door but had yet to climb in, just stood there looking at that swampside house over the roof of Gus' car.

"What are thinking?" she asked me.

"Oh, you know," I told her. "Just wondering if hell's hot."

ii

The Dismal Swamp was slightly west of Detective Colby's jurisdiction, but if he could scoop up a wrongful death suspect and send her back across the state, he guessed he could stand to drive out to Suffolk to meet me.

We ended up at a Sheetz on the fringes of the lot near the plug holes where the gas got delivered.

"All right," Colby said. "Let's hear it."

Dwight had worked up a pedigree on Sally Knighten. I gave a copy to Detective Colby and then set the scene for him.

"All right, then. Here's yours." He reached into his jacket pocket and pulled out some paper for me. "Three possibles for the Buckroe boyfriend. One of them's at Deerfield. Kidnap/abduction, malicious wounding. Other two have been off the grid for a while. I can't say for sure any of them hooked up with Abigail Tucker, but these are the only candidates I could find."

"Hearing anything on that Spotsylvania girl?"

Colby squinted the way cops do when they're pretending to try to remember a thing they've never actually heard of.

"Dead in the woods," I told him. "She was also wearing a daisy ring."

In Colby's defense, he almost surely had plenty of dead whodunnits in Norfolk, so outside paperwork that came across his desk just piled up in a bin. I knew that sort of situation, had been in worse myself. You were fighting a tide and always losing, so you watched where you were facing, didn't bother with side to side.

I passed Colby's info along to Dwight and then worked my shifts with Benny and soldiered through a week and a half of Gus-less nights at home. She'd gone back to Jeremy. She did that every now and then. Sometimes for an afternoon. Once for nearly three whole weeks. He'd start in with calls and texts, and then he'd usually come begging in person. I'd know he was devoted to the effort when he'd haul their son along.

Little Jeremy was one of those kids who hadn't heard "Shut your yap" nearly enough. It was easier to indulge him. Big Jeremy did it instinctively since he'd long been the same sort of creature, so that left Gus to put the brakes on, and she wasn't built for that.

The little Jeremy who'd come visit his mom (usually in my back yard at the elaborate jungle gym that had come with the house) had been bribed and primed to be on good behavior and make like he was missing his mother in an agonized and pitiful way. He could even pull it off, sometimes for a quarter hour, before he'd decide he'd met his obligation and more than held up his end.

Then little Jeremy would revert. He'd pout and sneer and whine, but Gus would go back home anyway because guilt is potent stuff. Of course, she got pressure from the mother-in-law as well. The woman would call every now and then and threaten to ruin Gus entirely. She'd do it in that chatty way that sounds like benign conversation with the poison buried in the piffle like a viper in a basket of lace. It got to Gus even though, truth be told, she was probably ruining things well enough without any help . Gus was living with a disgraced cop who drove a loan shark for money, and they shared a house in a part of Suffolk where decent people rarely went.

I never tried to talk Gus out of going home since we both seemed to know she'd come back. It was a mortifying ritual for her as much as anything. She'd fight off leaving until her regret required some kind of outlet, and the first couple of times she even made a show of taking all her stuff. Since then she'd gotten it down to a carry-on bag because it had become clear to her that life with her Jeremys wasn't likely to last.

I prefer to think I was healthy about it all. I had years of mistakes with women behind me, and while I'd hardly been a quick learner, I knew it would have been foolish to cling. I had faith that Gus would salve her conscience and then come on back my way. In time I expected she'd go for a visit without even a change of clothes.

So I ended up with ten days on my own. That was a lengthy stretch for Gus, but little Jeremy broke his collarbone and so actually needed his mother. He'd hadn't fallen off his scooter and or gotten injured playing Lacrosse but had gone for a joyride in his father's T-bird. A sixty-five landau. Mint. A neighbor up the road had a life-sized cement elk in his yard, and Jeremy had veered off the pavement, run through a hedge, and hit the thing.

He broke the front axle and took a chunk out of the elk. Cut his lip open and fractured his clavicle. A lot of mischief for an eleven-year-old, and on top of it all, he was drunk. The whole business got blamed on Gus, of course, her being the absent mother and all.

She called me. That was not at all her habit. Ordinarily, I wouldn't hear from her until she'd had her fill and had come back.

"How wretched am I?" she wanted to know.

"Can you give me a for instance?"

She told me the entire Thunderbird story.

"Your cooking's awful, and you can be a little pissy sometimes."

That was better than she'd hoped for. "Thanks," she said.

"Box came for you."

"Pink ones," she told me and hung up.

They were pink. She'd bought a dozen pair, had kind of an underpants habit, but then Gus did routinely sport them as outerwear and tended to rough them up. I shoved them all in her drawer, broke down her box, went back to my book and my whiskey, didn't feel enough of a twinge to spoil my night.

Gus didn't get back in time for the trip we'd planned to Chincoteague. It was all Dwight's doing. I was driving and lending some ex-cop patina to the meeting he'd arranged with BullittBoy27. Dwight had cultivated a kind of relationship with him, which had started with wide-ranging paranoid DM chatter that had narrowed to our dead girls in the woods.

It was two solid hours, across the narrows of the Chesapeake on the bridge tunnel and then up the Delmarva on thirteen almost to the Maryland line. Once we'd cleared the causeway and reached the island, Dwight directed me to the house, which had the unfortunate distinction of being nowhere near the water. A small ranch on a puny lot in an uncomely Chincoteague suburb. You couldn't even smell the brine from there.

"You doing the talking?" I asked Dwight on the way to the door.

He said he would and looked primed to until BullittBoy's mother answered. Janet. She was in her forties and wearing some kind of uniform. It turned out she waited tables in a motel restaurant. She looked tired, maybe closer to weary with its grinding moral component.

"Guess you're them," she and let us in as she was going out.

"Ev," she shouted. "They're here," and instructed us, "Don't lock it." Then she was off the porch and into her coupe in the yard.

Ev came rolling out and had a look at us. Bandana headband, sweatsuit, shower shoes and fingerless gloves. His wheelchair had decals all over it, most of them cannabis or gun related . I didn't get the feeling BullittBoy27 would be saving the whales.

"Hey," Dwight said.

Ev told him, "Hey."

Dwight pointed at me.

I got a head jerk. Then he wheeled around and left us to follow or not.

Ev's bedroom put our command center to shame. The kid had a world of equipment. He'd built all his computers, had monitors all over the place on all kinds of mounts and swivels so he could turn them how he pleased. Dwight was impressed, and he and Ev spent a quarter hour or so just talking components. Then Ev broke off for a look at me.

"What do you know about him?" he asked.

"He's all right. Used to be a cop somewhere."

"Lot of somewhere's," Ev told him and pointed at a stack of papers on his junky bed. Dwight picked it up. I saw my academy photo on the top.

Dwight had a look at the stuff and then tried to hand it to me. I shook my head and told him, "I was there."

I could guess what he'd come to soon enough.

"He know?" Ev asked me.

I shook my head.

"Think he ought to?"

"Probably."

Dwight was looking back and forth between us now. I was content to let Bullittboy take it from there.

"Your man here killed a girl himself."

Dwight went back to flipping pages. "Yeah. D.C.. 2007."

"How long have you known?" I asked him.

Dwight shrugged. "A while."

"Tell it," Ev said. "Let's hear it from you."

So there I was getting pushed around by some Chincoteague Island hacker who wore his bandana like a pirate and had a sticker on his wheelchair that said FEDS out of DIXIE!. Of course I wanted to fill him in on the darkest day of my life.

"I got detailed to treasury. We were sitting on a guy. Estonian. He was in the exotic bird biz. Worked out of a place in Lincoln Park, over near the armory."

"What birds?" Dwight asked.

"The endangered kind. People collect any damn thing, and he had some big-ticket customers. That's who we were really after."

"Yeah, and . . ." BullittBoy was rocking and balancing on his back wheelchair tires.

I was taking a dislike to the fellow, disability notwithstanding.

"They sent us in to pick him up. Feliks with a 'k'. We decided to just knock on the door and ask him to come along."

"Hiccup?"

"You're really losing me," I told Ev.

His snort was just like Dwight's. "It's a gift."

"Yeah, hiccup. He went out the back. We had to chase him. Then the fool started shooting at us.

Big soccer stadium over there. He headed in that direction. There was a game on, and I guess he was figuring to mix with the crowd. We were trying to cut him off. He got panicky. Fired again. I returned fire. Hit him." I laid a finger to the spot below my ribcage where my bullet had entered. "Went straight through. A girl rode by on her bike, and the slug caught her in the thigh. Nicked an artery. We applied pressure. Had her stable. Ambulance came. She died on the way."

I stopped talking. They waited on me.

"Twenty-one years old. Joyce Sparks."

"Trying to set things right?" Ev asked me. "That what this is about?"

I thought about the bottles I'd emptied. All the wandering I'd done. I shook my head. "There's no making that ok."

That worked for him. "All right then." Ev turned to his keyboard, told us, "Two dead girls. 2002 and 2012. Same kind of rings. No identical but, you know, black-eyed Susans."

And with that the BullittBoy litany started. He was confident, facile, glib. He could tell you hard facts and preposterous junk and make them both sound true. It was all in the delivery, crisp and certain. He'd behave like the stuff he was saying was obvious and irreproachable. Then he'd move on to the next thing while your brain was telling you, "Wait. What?"

It was a good thing there were two of us. Dwight slowed him down with process talk, an ongoing inquisition about data banks and algorithms, which left me free to check the various screens and bone up on case details. Ev appeared to have chased down every scrap of Spotsylvania evidence and even had some Abigail Tucker stuff we'd never seen.

"Got hard copies?"

"Some."

Ev handed them over to me. I retired to the kitchen and sat at the table there to read while the boys talked case details and tech Ev had used to find them. I could hear them in there. Ev, smug and sure. Dwight, tentative but (in my experience) thorough and incisive.

"So?" Ev asked as I reentered his lair.

"Lot of duplicates. What else you got?"

"Forensics on the Spotsylvania girl."

Ev tapped a few keys and pulled up the county coroner's preliminary report and notes. Photos too.

Dwight leaned in to read the screen "Strangled," he said. "Interfered with, but they're not sure with what."

That coroner was thorough. Between her notes and her report, she didn't appear to have missed a thing. The victim was fifteen and four months, seven days. Her final meal was pizza and french fries. She'd been a cutter, scars on her inner thighs. COD was ligature strangulation, possibly with a rope. The interference was all post mortem, and the coroner had made a list of implements that might have been used in the act.

"You ever been arrested for this stuff?" I asked Ev.

"Define 'arrested'."

"Read your rights. Booked. Bailed. Like that."

Ev shook his head. "Got talked to twice. State and federal. Some DDOS thing, but we all decided it wasn't me."

"That it?" Dwight had done a work up for me.

"The stalking? That what you after?"

I nodded.

"It wasn't like . . . romantic, you know." Another wheelie.

Me and Dwight waited.

"Met her at church."

That earned a special involuntary necknoise from Dwight. Who in the world went to church?

"My mom used to make me. Had this phase where she was done with doctors but high on Jesus until He let her down too."

More waiting.

"The girl seemed all right. So I made a few . . . inquiries."

Dwight was sympathetic. He was an inquisitive son-of-a-gun himself.

"Might have dug too deep," Bullittboy allowed. "A couple of cops came around."

"What makes you think they're not watching you now?" I asked him.

"Probably are," Ev said. "That me anyway." He pointed at an old Mac desktop shunted off in a corner. "Over there I'm playing Witcher, surfing porn."

"A crawler?" Dwight asked.

Ev nodded. "My own."

That was something Dwight needed to hear about, and he pressed Ev for details, so I took the stack of forensic goods and retired to the kitchen once more.

Julie Fay Greer didn't look fifteen dead. She looked twenty easy, and with some mileage. Pubic hair shaved into a strip. Quite a lot of tattoos for a minor, and not seahorses and unicorns but spider webs and scaly dragons and skulls, along with a gothic thing up her left thigh — just the word 'Evermore'. She had needle marks and all kinds of ligature bruising, old and new, neck and wrists.

In one photograph was all the hardware they'd removed from her ears and nose. They'd found traces of opioids in her blood. She'd had a pregnancy terminated and an appendectomy. Fifteen, four months, seven days.

The coroner had speculated in her notes more than coroners usually do. She'd worked through possibilities on the victim's cause of death. Asphyxiation for sure, but orgasmic hypoxia seemed like a legitimate option, given where the bruising was most severe. The corner had set down a lively description of asphyxiophilia practices that wasn't dry at all, more of an enthusiast's take.

By the time I got back to the bedroom, those boys had made a few decisions.

"He's coming with us," Dwight said.

"What?"

Ev had shoved some stuff in a gym bag and pointed at it on the floor.

"Coming where exactly?" I asked Dwight.

"He can stay with me."

"What about your mom?" Dwight shrugged. "And your mom?"

"She knows. She's cool."

"You sure about this?"

Dwight nodded.

"Fine," I said. I asked Ev, "Do you need meds or something?"

Ev shook his head. "I'm clean." He pointed at his computer on the floor in the corner. "But he's on all kinds of shit."

Ev was heavier than he looked, and I was fearful of twisting him wrong until he barked at me when I left off caring. All the way back south he browsed on his laptop in the front passenger seat.

"Cop up here," he told me more than once, and he was never wrong.

We stopped for chicken tacos and ibuprofen, and everyplace we went, Ev had to come as well. That meant wheelchair wrangling and some dead lifting, but I couldn't really blame him for wanting to actually be out in the world. Ev had a way with the girls, got one's number at a Walgreen's. They all pitied him just enough to allow him an in.

"Can't waste the crip," he told us. He needed a sticker that said that.

Ev insisted on inspecting our nerve center before going over to Dwight's, so we all went in my house, and Gus was back. Her bag was on the sofa, and she was sitting in front of the whiteboard. She'd hung her pants on the doorknob and came out to see what all the racket was about.

"Underwear lady!" Ev liked what he saw. "I was afraid y'all'd busted up."

"Let me guess," Gus said. "You brought the bullittboy."

iii

Vilmer Demarest had an episode. That's what
they said at the nurse's station when I didn't find
him in his dead end piece of hall. They'd moved
him to the special-care part of the place, so I
dropped by the Rhododendron Hills Solarium
and grabbed Gus on my way to Vilmer's bedside.

She was talking to twins. They were ninety-
something and catty, still did up their hair every
day and wore proper dresses instead of house
coats. They'd both married bomber pilots and
had both raised ungrateful kids. Neither one of
them knew what she would do without her daily
dose of sherry. Gus had peeled off and zeroed in
on them as we were walking by because she had a
good instinct for who was worth her time.

"This your man?" one of them asked as I swung
by to pick her up.

Gus managed a nod and a, "Maybe." They all
cackled like I figured they would.

Vilmer Demarest smelled better than Uncle
Homer ever had, but he sure seemed to be just as
sleepy. He was sharing a room with another man
who was reading the Richmond paper.

"Pull the curtain if you want," he told us.

We didn't. "He ever awake?" I asked.

He shook his head. "Groans some."

"Know what happened?"

"Stroke, they said." He folded his paper and laid it aside. "Guess you're not his people."

"Just friends," Gus told him. "Met him here."

"Come meet me here." He stuck out his hand. Gus went and took it. He was Floyd from Williamsburg.

"How are you doing?" she asked.

"Had some kind of something. Mostly old and bored."

"Ever know him awake?" I pointed at Mr. Demarest.

Floyd nodded. "Jawed with him a few times. Used to run a grocery store, I think."

"Sunoco."

"That's it," he told me. "Had a girl that died. He talked about her some."

Gus perched on the side of Floyd's bed. "Abigail?" she said.

Floyd nodded. "Ate him up. Can't blame him, but who needs to hear that all day?"

"Did he say what happened to her?" I asked him,

"Sick, I guess."

Then I gave Gus the head jerk and retired to the doorway.

"You," Floyd told Gus exclusively, "can come around whenever you want." I only got a wink and a gummy grin.

We were out in the lot and about to the car when Gus said the very thing I'd been thinking: "So she was his kid then."

"Could be. Let's put the nerd herd on it."

"Would it matter?" she asked.

"Make him more than just a snoopy crank."

The history Dwight and Ev dug up was colorful but inconclusive. Mr. Vilmer Demarest, as it turned out, was once an ambitious horndog. They found photos of him as a forty-something rascal. He was fit and blonde, clothes hung well on him. He'd been written up over in Newport News when he opened a car lot there, not a regular lot but some whacked-out venture that sold pre-owned luxury sedans and made their own glazed doughnuts, which they handed out to anybody who swung by for a browse.

It didn't catch on, apparently, and was described as 'failed' in a subsequent article about an assault where Vilmer Demarest had been the beatee and the victim. He'd taken liberties with a woman who was another gentleman's wife. It sounded like she'd taken liberties as well, but

Vilmer was the news because her husband had thumped him with a table lamp and there was worry of lingering brain damage. The article featured a photo of Vilmer Demarest's pulpy face.

Dwight blew it up and put it on the corkboard with one of the Cadillac push pins. Mr. Demarest almost didn't look human, was nearly too cracked open and swollen to pass for a man.

"What happened after?" I asked them.

"Sunoco," Ev told us and pulled up mostly a bunch of advertisements, but a photo had run in some sort of rag of the station's grand opening, and there was Vilmer Demarest recovered and smiling and looking like a horndog again.

"And Abigail Tucker?" Gus asked.

"Might be his," Dwight said.

"Think he felt guilty?" Ev asked. "Her getting dead and all?"

"As good a reason to care as any," I told him and had a look at both dead girls — Abigail Tucker with her freckles and green eyes and Julie Fay Greer looking pinched and troubled and nearly (in the snapshot the boys had dug up) like I child. "Hell, I care about them, and they're not even mine."

I pulled a couple of days with Benny that week, and one of them got dicey for me. He had me stop at the Norfolk magistrate's office.

"Got a thing," was all he said.

I went where he told me. Parked on St. Paul, and then we just sat and waited. "Picking up an associate," he informed me and then asked for Giulio Cesare.

"Here he is," Benny said after about a quarter hour. He shoved his back door open, and I glanced over to see swampside Leonard coming out to the car.

He had a woman with him, a lawyer it turned out. She was a leathery thing, all legalese and elbows. They stopped ten yards from the curb so she could give Leonard confidential instruction — everything he ought to avoid getting up to, all he shouldn't say.

She talked. He nodded ever so slightly. Leonard's white shirt and trousers were wrinkled, liked he'd slept in them in a cell.

Benny noticed me watching the pair of them. "Spot of trouble," he explained.

I gave him the nod that was customary for me, the one that meant "Thanks. Not my business."

I hadn't come up with a workable response to what I expected to hear from Leonard beyond, "Hey, buddy, you've got me mixed up with somebody else."

It wouldn't serve. He'd be insistent. I'd get a taste of Benny's dogwood staff.

The lawyer finally finished with Leonard, and he got into the car. Benny pointed my way and made the introductions. I caught Leonard's gaze in the mirror and waited for that flash of recognition, but he just grunted at me and fell into telling Benny about the charges he faced. It sounded like Colby had hit him with some low-level possession beef.

Benny had me carry Leonard to the swampside house once we'd stopped on the way for groceries. I got sent in to pick up canned soup, a bag of apples, and honey grahams.

Once we reached the house, Leonard asked if I'd carry the groceries inside. I did. I set the bag on the kitchen counter. The front door frame was splintered. The furniture was upset. The TV was screen-down on the floor and busted. It looked like SWAT had stormed in and pretty much wrecked the place.

Leonard was waiting for me in the doorway as I headed back out. He smiled and laid a hand to my shoulder. "Hey, fuse man," he said. "Be seeing you soon."

Benny was none the wiser when I got back to the car. He gave me an address in Copeland, had a client he meant to concuss.

I told it all to Gus and the boys once I'd found them in our command center. They were talking about orgasms at the time. Gus anyway had been talking about them while Ev and Dwight had been sunning their molars.

I stepped in to save those boys a world of worry and trouble. "Just do what you're told," I said.

Then it was on to Leonard and my chunk of afternoon.

"I guess he's got some use for you," was the way that Ev distilled it.

"That's what I'm afraid of. Need to know more about him than I do."

So Dwight and Ev went scouring for everything they could find. Norfolk booking records for starters. Leonard was a Musgrove, a lot of arrests but no convictions that either of the boys could find. Witnesses forgetting their stories. Evidence walking away.

"Strange bird," Gus said as she studied a Leonard booking photo that captured the stern and preacherly look of the man. Starched white shirt buttoned up to the throat. Hair slicked back. Eyes little short of black. Far more flinty Old Testament to him than modern, warm-blooded humanity.

I'd seen a guy or two like that in my working life, the sort who'd gone around the corner and lived beyond any kind of appeal you could usually make to a child of God.

"Snitch." That's how I read him.

Everything was transactional for a man like Leonard. He'd clearly decided he had use for me or he would have burned me with Benny already. And given the way Benny treated him, he must have had something on him as well.

"Do some digging on Benny," I said to the boys. "But be careful. He's got people."

"IT people?" Dwight asked.

Person anyway. His name was Orin, and he specialized in forensic spreadsheet stuff, but he sniffed around more generally for Benny as well to see who was showing an interest. Local law enforcement. Federal agents. Russians maybe too.

The boys started out by going deep on Leonard and worked up a dossier. The man was a Texan by birth. Nederland, almost Louisiana, where he'd had trouble as a juvenile. Some kind of animal cruelty thing that seemed to have involved a pony, though the details were mostly sealed.

"Galveston prep for bad boys," Dwight told me. "Then two years in the National Guard. Some kind of moral rehab."

"Didn't take," Ev said. He pointed me to an arrest report he'd pulled up on his laptop screen. "Baton Rouge. Crime against nature. They're a little vague on the particulars, but the statute says, 'Marriage to, or sexual intercourse with, any ascendant or descendant, brother or sister, uncle or niece, aunt or nephew, with knowledge of their relationship'."

"What else?" I asked.

"Ohio," Dwight told me. He had a screen to point me to as well. "Columbus. Pandering and loitering."

"Fraud charges. Fairfax County." This was Ev. "Also aggravated indecent assault. Easton, PA. 2010. Victim was unconscious."

"Female?" I asked.

"Trixie," Ev told me. "So . . . yes?"

"He ever do time?" I asked.

"Probation." Ev again.

"Lots of probation," Dwight added.

So definitely a snitch. " Where does Benny come in?" I asked them.

"Don't know yet," Dwight told me.

"Guess maybe I'll go see Leonard since that seems to be what he wants."

Gus insisted I take my gun, the old Ruger I kept wrapped in a golf towel in the nightstand drawer. I humored her, but Leonard wasn't the sort you shot. He was an outrage magnet, a man so indecent he had to be pulverized, weighed down with rocks, and dropped in a pond somewhere. Leonard's type demanded obliteration. A bullet wouldn't be nearly enough, and this was really just a meet and greet. Social and exploratory.

I didn't bother to make any sort of a plan but just drove out to the Dismal Swamp and parked in the yard of that moldering house, avoided the dog, and mounted the porch. The door was standing half open, the frame still splintered from the battering ram. I went straight on in. Nothing had been tidied or set right.

There were books on the floor in the far corner where the cops had tipped over a cabinet. I had a look at them in hopes of getting a better a sense of Leonard, but he seemed to be the sort who'd read just about anything. Philosophy. Science. Valley of the Dolls. A campaign tome by a congressman who'd been dead for at least a decade. A quiche cookbook. Edna St. Vincent Millay's sonnets. Number four in the Sunshine Series! devoted to how to build a deck.

Leonard had joined me without my knowing it. "Here he is," he said. "Come." He turned and left. I followed.

We went down the gloomy hallway and into the gloomy kitchen. It was neat. Clean even, and not just tidy but scoured and smelling fresh.

"Tea?"

"No thanks."

He had a kettle on a burner and a mug on the counter with a tea ball in it. Leonard kept touching the kettle to check the temperature and filled his cup just as it whistling started. He pointed at the dinette. We both stepped over and sat.

Leonard studied me while he dunked his tea ball. "You gave up the girl? Is that how it went?"

"Pretty much."

"Why?"

"Trading up."

"For what?"

"Needed some files. Looking into a cold case." The truth, or something close to it, seemed like the best course of action with Leonard. He had that slow, deceitful metabolism that could easily wait out a lie.

"You try asking for them?"

I nodded. "Tit for tat. You know how works with cops."

His tea was just right the color for him, so he shifted the ball to a saucer. "Just as well. She was kind a problem, that girl. Not an ounce of self-control."

"Glad to help."

Leonard smiled as she shot the contents of his mug right onto my frontside. Soaked my shirt mostly, got my neck a little. Hot enough to be uncomfortable but not to blister skin. I was standing up and sputtering when Leonard hit me with a saucepan. A shitty piece of Revere Ware he'd reached over and grabbed casually off the stove. It was too thin and light to do terribly much damage, but it made a hell of a lot of racket and stunned me sufficiently that the linoleum seemed inviting, so I sat.

While I was there, Leonard took occasion to kick me twice. Not viciously but with a kind of clinical precision so that the toe of his shoe hit both times in the exact same tender spot.

Then he gave me a pat on the head and helped me up. Sat me back in my chair.

"How about I make you a cup?"

"Sure," I told him. He did, and I failed to throw it on him.

Leonard broke out a sleeve of sugar cookies and told me at length about a pileated woodpecker he'd seen.

"The swamp," I remember him saying, "is a refuge for me."

That made sense since he was part reptile. I finally asked him, "What do you need?"

"Benny," he said.

"What about him?"

"I'd like . . . insight."

I shrugged. "I just drive him a couple of days a week."

"You'll be my ears."

I shrugged. "Kind of dull. People pay him or wish they had."

"Let's say Tuesdays."

Then he rose from the table, and I followed him back along the hall. I lingered on the front porch while Leonard stood in the shattered doorway. We probably looked like regular people capping off a cordial chat.

"Two-ish. Here's good."

I nodded. "Ask you something?"

He nodded.

"Mags. Benny's girl."

He nodded again.

"I'm curious. How'd you tame her?"

Leonard raised his right index finger and showed me his yellow incisors. "Excellence," he said, "is not an act, but a habit."

I dodged the nasty dog in the yard and went back to my car.

iv

I don't like complicated, have a long-held preference for simple and spare, but there I was with entanglements in nearly every direction. Leonard, Benny, Mags (I guess), two dead girls, another man's wife for a lady friend, a nerdling neighbor boy, and a paraplegic on a visit. I hadn't even wanted a job driving Benny, was just doing him a favor because Marco got in Dutch.

Now I was supposed to spy on the guy? Benny was scrupulously unrevealing, and Leonard hadn't bothered to clue me in on what he wanted to know. Benny wasn't chatty by nature on account of his CP, so he chose his spots and told me little or nothing in moist bursts.

Benny lived modestly three doors down. Thanks to Leonard, Benny had a docile girlfriend, but she only seemed to come around a couple of nights a week. He got his Chrysler detailed every other month — a guy came to his house to do it — and occasionally Benny cooked out on a big brick grill at the bottom of his yard. Burgers exclusively since they were no challenge to mash up.

Benny watched satellite TV and collected vacuum-tube stereo equipment. Orin (his IT department) would swing by once a quarter or so, and they'd run through accounts at Benny's dining room table. Benny had me carry him to church once — a big Episcopalian eyesore — but I got the feeling he'd gone there to threaten the priest rather than seek counsel or pray.

When I explained the task ahead of me to Gus and Dwight and Ev, Ev asked me, "Why don't you just kill him?"

"Leonard?"

All three of them nodded like that would be nothing, maybe an afternoon's diversion.

We were having supper in my kitchen. It was something we did once or twice a week, chiefly to give a break to Dwight's mom, who was still trolling the web for romance. Those meals were nothing close to a treat because either Gus would make her tamales — thaw and heat them anyway — or I'd throw together one of my casseroles (constipation with melted cheese). We usually added value with the sort of talk actual families rarely allow. One of our previous suppers had seen Gus make an IUD mock up with flexi drink straws and corkscrew pasta. Those boys had an awful lot of questions about sex.

"Have y'all killed anybody?" I asked them.

"In my heart," Gus said.

"No bleeders there," I told her.

"Two in the hat. You've got the hardware." That from Ev.

Dwight added, "Yeah."

It was tamale night. Mine was still frozen in the middle. I showed the chunk of frosty filling to Gus who huffed and snatched my plate, nuked the thing a minute more to make it incendiary, which would shut me up for sure.

"Something's going on with Benny. Something Leonard cares about." I told Ev and Dwight, "I need you two on it."

"I've got a test," Dwight said.

It was easy to forget that Dwight was fifteen and had school to go to and kid stuff to do.

"I'm on it," Ev told me mostly. Then he said to Gus, "My shit's still frozen."

She huffed. She snatched. She made his molten too.

So on my days I drove Benny, I listened hard, since it wasn't like he was remotely the sort to tolerate getting peppered with questions. He made calls and took calls, issued his usual advisements, which meant cover the vig or take your sutures. Benny liked it simple and spare as well.

One day when Mags was along, I passed a
quarter hour with her while Benny wrangled with
a client. The guy was a regular, and his excuses
were elaborate and unpersuasive. He was sure to
get smacked, but Benny always did him the
courtesy of hearing him out first.

We were parked in a shopping plaza. The client
ran a jewelry store in a part of Norfolk that didn't
buy jewelry anymore but just stole it and pawned
it. Then the cops would come pick it up. So the
guy was in a bit of a tight spot that Benny had
helped make tighter. Me and Mags sat at a table
at the kabob place two doors down.

"Want something to eat?" I asked. I was having
silty coffee and some kind of honey-soaked
pastry.

She shook her head. Said nothing. That was a
big change from old Mags who had rarely left
much of anything uncommented upon.

"You all right?" I just threw it out there in a
general way, so if she was having a crisis of faith
or her shoes were too tight it would apply either
way.

Mags gave me an apprising look. That was one
of her specialties. From the beginning, she'd been
the type inclined to size people up with a glance,
though early on you got the feeling she was
looking for your soft spot, somewhere she could

burrow in and make you sorry you were weak.
This was a different Mags, more looking to see if
I'd turn on and betray her, if I was the type to
keep a confidence or pass it right along.

"Been better."

I sipped my coffee, picked at my sweet. "That
place we picked you up," I said, "Swampside . . . ."
This was treacherous territory. Mags watched me
and waited. I'm pretty sure neither one of us
knew what I'd say next. "You came out a little
different."

That earned me a snorty laugh.

I glanced towards the jewelry store. No sign of
Benny, no sound yet of violence.

"The guy out there, Leonard, dresses like a
preacher . . . "

Mags nodded.

"We fetched him from jail the other day.
What's his story?"

Mags got quivery for a moment, couldn't seem
to help it.

"Sorry, I didn't mean to . . . ." I was doing that
man thing where you toss a grenade and then act
like you have qualms about it.

Mags glanced at the jewelry shop door. "What
did he tell you?" She meant Benny.

"Nothing. I drive. I change his CDs. Mash up
his lunch. Like that."

Mags passed a moment just looking at me, made her determination. "They . . . persuaded me."

I heard a raised voice from the jewelry shop. The client, probably pleading.

"To do what?"

"Get right, you know, with Jesus."

There was now an authentic uproar coming from the jewelry shop. Stuff breaking. A grown man shouting.

"Benny likes stuff a certain way," she told me. "I see that now."

The front jewelry store window shattered as a bronze lamp passed through it. A nymph on a rock. She bounced across the sidewalk and ended up face down in the fire lane. Benny followed her. He used the door and told us both with his customary extra spit, "Let's go."

I told Gus about my conversation with Mags in the middle of the night, hoped she'd be armed with insights I'd never know as a man.

"It's that Pygmalion thing," she told me, "but with closed fists and strangulation."

"Sounds like it worked."

"Why wouldn't it?"

Ev apparently didn't sleep any better than we did and spent his small hours scouring the

internet for anything pertinent he could find. He
came rolling up first thing in the morning and
gave me a shout from the front walk so I'd go
outside and drag him backwards onto the stoop
and into the house.

"Wasn't even looking for this," he told me as he
fished his laptop out of his bag. I got the usual
whiff of vaporizer and Doritos.

Ev opened his computer and showed me a
booking photo on the screen. White guy. Mid-
thirties with red hair and freckles. Scowl. Dull,
vermin gaze.

"Ranger Randy Pyle," he said. Pyle had been
arrested in Martinsburg for grand larceny in
2006. "Him and a buddy stole a bunch of guns."

"He still inside?"

"Not sure. Thing is, you know the buddy."

Ev pulled up another photo. A swarthy young
man I needed a moment to recognize. He'd
changed quite a lot in a decade, was skinnier back
then, sallow and druggy. The version I knew had
cleaned up and muscled out.

"Marco?"

Ev nodded.

"Have I told you how much I hate a
coincidence?"

Ev nodded and said, "Yep."

My mind was sifting through the facts we'd
gathered, the evidence layered on our corkboard,
which had been mostly loose and unrelated, just
stuff you picked up and clung to in the general
course of sniffing around. That was case work all
over. You filled your book with details and
worked up theories to make as many of them fit
and adhere as you could. It was usually an
artificial exercise, particularly with a case as cold
as ours. You hoped you'd find a suspect with a
troubled conscience and a Biblical sense of
justice, a nagging appetite for moral balance in
this world. What you usually got was a bunch of
useless bits and bobs from an evidence locker and
witnesses who had forgotten most pertinent
things they'd ever known.

Gus came in while I was sitting and settling. Ev
showed her Marco on her screen.

"Who's this?"

"Benny's regular guy," I told her.

"He's got a Simmons Gap connection," Ev said.

"How long's he been working for Benny?" Gus
asked.

I didn't know and shook my head.

"Has he got a kink on?" Ev wanted to know.

I wouldn't have guessed it, but who could say.
Marco could have killed those girls if they'd both
cut him off on the freeway.

"We need to find Ranger Randy," I said.

"Working on it," Ev told me back.

Randy Pyle was proving difficult to pin down. He'd done his time in West Virginia and then had jumped parole. There was no record of him anywhere that Ev could find. No arrests. No taxes filed. No DMV sign up. His social had gone dormant.

"So he's dead or different," I told the boys, once we'd all assembled.

Dwight took dead; Ev took different. Me and Gus, for our part, decided on sort of a flyer and rode out to Rhododendron Hills to see if Vilmer had come around.

He had, a little. He was recovered enough to sit out in his old piece of hallway, but in a wheelchair and wrapped in a linty, waffle-weave blanket. He was getting glucose or something in one arm and had a monitor clip on his opposite index finger. Vilmer wasn't looking at the fire alarm when we found him.

"Mr. Demarest." That didn't reach him.

Gus laid a hand to Vilmer's bony wrist and rubbed until he'd shifted a bit and finally looked her way.

"Hey," she said.

He made a noise.

"Remember him?" She pointed at me.

Vilmer took me in with his watery eyes and made a noise again. I pulled out the stuff I'd brought — booking and forensic photos that the boys had printed for me, while Gus used a corner of Mr. Demarest's blanket to blot away his drool.

I started with Marco's mugshot, which Vilmer very nearly looked at before he grunted and turned away.

"Try Abigail," Gus said. "We're sure of her."

We had one decent posed shot of Abigail Tucker live and unmurdered, which I slipped into the general area where Vilmer Demarest was staring. He made a racket that sounded like talking and reached for the picture with his waxy hand. I let him have it. He told us a few things further, but Vilmer couldn't form his words. We just got throaty noises and leaking spit.

"Ranger Randy," Gus suggested.

I plucked Randy Pyle's booking shot free and put it where Mr. Demarest could see it. He stared. He focused. I think he moaned.

"You know him?"

I let Gus handle it. Vilmer clearly preferred her to me.

He warbled, I'll call it. Made a complicated, throaty noise.

"That's a yes?" she said.

He nodded and reached out a hand for Gus to
take and hold.

"Know him from Chuckatuck? Sunoco? Like
that?" she asked.

That didn't result in the nod I'd hoped for.
More warbling, like he knew Randy Pyle from
somewhere that needed explaining.

"Ideas?" Gus asked me.

"Did you talk to him?" I said to Vilmer, "back
when you were sniffing around?"

I got more or less a "Yes" for that, a clearly
affirmative burst of spit and racket. Gus and I
consulted with now what? glances.

She did some more hand rubbing to keep Mr.
Demarest engaged. And partially erect as it
turned out. That linty blanket didn't hide much,
so we both got a peek at Vilmer Demarest's
tribute to horndoggery.

"Tuck him in," Gus instructed me.

"You tuck him in."

It was our usual sort of standoff, which meant I
yielded and pulled out my Bic pen and rearranged
Vilmer's pajamas.

I'd decided we were done, had ridden all the
way over to Rhododendron Hills just to find out
that Vilmer Demarest had been aware of Randy
Pyle, but Gus wasn't about to be stopped by that
gentleman's limitations, and she kept hovering

close and quizzing him, pawing at him when he'd drift.

"What are you hoping for here? A dinner date?"

I know now Gus was right to ignore me. She got drool and sinusy noises for a while but one nugget of useful, semi-articulate business in the end.

Vilmer Demarest made a racket that sounded like something, nearly like a word.

"One more time," Gus told him and rubbed him up good for incentive.

I could see Mr. Demarest sort of gather himself, half wanting to tell us a useful thing, half needing Gus to be pleased.

He made the same noise again but with more definition to it.

"Is that Saluda?" I asked.

"Could be. Is that a thing?"

"Place. Saluda, Virginia?"

Vilmer's grunt was a definitive Yes.

"That where he's from? Randy Pyle?"

I got a nod from Vilmer Demarest.

"You ought to hug him or something," I told Gus.

She looked where I was looking. Little Vilmer had gone eager again.

"Road trip," Ev told us back at the house.

The boys were working on Pyles and Pyle relations in and around the town of Saluda.

"What are you finding?" I asked.

"Six or eight of them," Dwight said. "A bunch more north of town, up near the Rappahannock."

"Where's this place exactly?" Gus wanted to know.

Ev pulled up a map and showed her Saluda, on a finger of land north of Mobjack Bay.

"That's like . . . close," she said.

I was the two-day-a-week professional driver, so they all turned to me. "Hour and a half with traffic."

Ev's cell rang. He glanced at the screen and killed the call. His mom again. He kept not talking to her, but now I felt like I had him.

"Call her back or you're staying here," I told Ev.

That earned me a Vilmer quality necknoise, but he made the call.

Understandably, Ev's mother thought she wanted to talk to me, but I knew she probably needed to talk to Gus and so made Ev give her his phone instead.

Gus said, "Hey," and left the room.

"So what' the deal?" I asked Ev.

"She's always on me. Gets old."

"She calls, you answer, tell her you're fine. She gets off you a little. Why make it so hard?"

Gus came back in and gave Ev his phone.

"Tell her you love her," she told him. It wasn't a suggestion.

Ev made a sour face, but Gus was an accomplished pincher and grabbed a hunk of tender skin. She just needed a thumb and forefinger's worth to make you quake and squirm.

Ev raised his phone to his ear and said, "Love ya." He listened, told his mom, "All right," and hung up.

"You're going to call her every other day." Ev hesitated until Gus showed him her finger and thumb. He nodded. "We need to get his meds," she told me.

"What meds?"

She'd written the name down and showed me her scrap of paper.

"What's it for?" I asked Ev who told me, "Stuff."

"And he's blogging about us," Gus informed me. "You know about this?" she asked Dwight.

Dwight shook his head in a way that said he certainly wished he didn't.

"Show us," I told him, and Dwight pulled up Ev's catty stream of commentary on his website. It was the usual blend of snark and misinformation but with phone photos that Ev had included as well. White-board stuff, me and

Dwight in conversation, Gus without her trousers walking away.

My impulse was to keep her from seeing it, but Ev had earned whatever was coming, and he got hung up on the door frame as he was trying to roll out of the room. That was all the help Gus needed, and she laid into him but good — half verbal harangue, half poking and pinching. She even smacked him once.

Ev kept telling her, "Wait!"

Gus wasn't feeling patient or even a little empathetic, and she took Ev's paraplegia as just a thing that made him more convenient.

Ev auditioned assorted excuses. He was feeling insecure and homesick. "I'm a kid. I'm rebelling," he told her.

Gus gave him a dope slap. "You're twenty-two."

For a second there, it looked like Ev was going to trot out, "I'm a cripple!", but I guess he thought better of it since the chances probably seemed good Gus would dump him on the floor and kick him around for a while.

Most educational experiences aren't worth much. You learn that, whatever you did, you wished you hadn't done it. This one was different since Gus was a woman who knew all about regret and had a true gift for inspiring it in others. The more Ev said, "Wait!" and "All right!" the more dedicated she grew.

Me and Dwight weren't about to interfere, though Ev kept glancing at us like there was some sort of brotherhood with codes and standards that we were sworn to live by and observe. No chance of that. Gus finally got tired, but by then she'd pinched Ev about everywhere she could reach and had left him looking like he'd fallen out with an octopus.

Ev was used to barking at his mother and telling unseen strangers ugly stuff on the web. He'd yet to get his proper bearings out in the actual world, and I like to think Gus was helping him along with that.

"Y'all are like fierce and shit," Ev finally told us.

That was good enough for Gus. She decided we could forgive him. Ev got a kiss up around his cowlick.

"Welcome, brother," Gus said.

Things Socratic

i

Saluda, Virginia, is nowhere much, south of the Rappahannock River, gateway to Deltaville, which is kind of nowhere squared. We showed up with a list of Pyles and an appointment at the Middlesex County courthouse where a woman named Millie helped us out in spite of what we were — two uncredentialed adults, one loud-mouth millennial in a wheelchair, and one teen we'd pulled out of school for the day. He was missing gym and something called World Portal.

"Why Pyles?" Millie wanted to know.

"Family tree stuff," Ev informed her. Then he dug a junky video camera out of his sack and said to Millie, "We're YouTubing it."

"Oh?"

Ev nodded. He wheeled in closer for a more confidential chat, and me and Gus and Dwight pulled back a touch so those two could have a moment.

Millie knew actual Pyles herself and claimed to have some memory of Ranger Randy. "Bony thing. His people come from up by Urbanna. Lived with an aunt. I'm pretty sure that was him."

"She still around?" Ev asked. Now he was videoing Millie.

"Think so." She knew what records to check and so did some scouring for us. She licked her lips and fixed her hair, jotted down an Urbanna address.

They had one of those old-timey Tastee Freezes on the north edge of Saluda that sold footlongs and a shake with Heath Bars in it, so we stopped off for a consult and a dose of gastric distress.

"What's the plan?" I asked and got the look I'd anticipated, not from any one of them but from all of them together. They didn't do plans but depended instead on free-form improvisation and occasionally even the homely truth. Plans like mine got me in Dutch with the Leonards of the world, and I was well aware of my personal history of considered schemes going sideways.

Dwight was working his way through a chili dog, had orange grease up to his eye sockets. Gus proved content to make a plan for him. "Diarrhea," she said.

It didn't turn out that way exactly, at least not immediately. Dwight just complained and gurgled all the way up to Urbanna where no amount of technology would help us find Ranger Randy's aunt's house. It turned out it had been bulldozed and the aunt had been shifted into a planned community called River View, even though you could only hope to see the Rappahannock if you climbed a tree.

The woman lived in a shoebox-shaped manufactured home like everybody else in the place. They all had holly bushes and nandinas, identical faux-colonial light posts, and cars parked (in the Virginia way) all over the damn place.

Randy Pyle's aunt was about to be on her way somewhere when we finally tracked her down. Book club, and they were supposed to have read Lord Jim, but Ranger Randy's aunt had only gotten through a third, and she'd been tapped at the last minute to lead the discussion because Evelyn, she informed us, had bailed.

"Phlebitis my ass," was how Ranger Randy's aunt put it.

"Big Lord Jim fan." I tapped my chest. "Fill you in if you give us a minute."

She unshouldered her pocketbook in her foyer and dropped it with a thump onto the floor.

It turned out Ranger Randy's aunt had married a small-engine repair guy name Murray who had squirreled away lots of untaxed cash through the years and had then conveniently died. She had a picture of him, a bleached out snapshot on a shelf by her sliding doors. Murray was stripped to the waist and holding a channel bass he'd pulled out of the Atlantic.

Gus was all set to say something consoling when Ranger Randy's aunt turned my way. "Tell me about that boat that didn't sink."

So I gave her some Lord Jim info and updated her on the Patna before breaking off and turning Gus and both boys loose to quiz her.

The woman had little use for her nephew, as it turned out. "Worthless," she explained.

"Didn't he work as a ranger?" Gus asked.

She nodded. "Way back. Hasn't drawn a decent check since. In and out of jail. Can't have nothing nice around him."

"Where is he now?" Ev asked.

Randy's aunt had a good long look and asked Ev, "What happened to you?"

"Car wreck. Dad was about half drunk, so don't tell me about worthless."

"Our Lord Jesus has a plan, and you're in it."

I felt better anyway. He didn't improvise either.

"Maybe," Ev said. "Randy first."

"Locked up," she told him.

"Where and for what?"

"Stealing. Like that."

"Ever any sex charges?" Gus asked. "Something rapey? Assault? That sort of thing?"

"Randy always liked the girls," she said, "a lot more than they liked him."

"Do any violence to any of them?" Ev again.

She gave it some thought and shook her head. "He's not mean, just sorry. If a girl wouldn't have him, he'd go steal her tires or something. What's this about?"

"Locked up where?"

"That place over by Culpeper," she told me.

Dwight looked it up on his phone. "Coffeewood?"

Ranger Randy's aunt nodded.

"Ever hear the name Abigail Tucker?" I asked her.

She shook her head and asked us again, "What's all this about?"

She didn't know Marco. Gus showed her a picture, and she was getting put out with us anyway.

"Can I use your bathroom?" We all looked at Dwight. He was sweating nearly everywhere he could be.

Randy's aunt pointed, and Dwight hustled off.

"Boat doesn't sink," I told the woman, holding up my end of the deal. "The Patna."

She was with me now and nodded.

"The passengers live. Crew saves themselves. Jim goes out in the wild with the natives to try to be righteous but ends up dead. When you get down to it, it's probably a book about shame."

Randy's aunt and Gus and Ev even all made the same sort of amused noise. I wasn't surprised. Shame's antique in this world, one of those things people only used to have like washboards or Victrolas.

We stopped and got Dwight some Pepto and picked up the vitamins Ev's mom had told Gus he needed to take, and then they lobbied me to drive straight out to Coffeewood and see Randy Pyle. Ev and Gus lobbied anyway while Dwight looked like a kid who would have preferred to go back in time, somewhere between breakfast and Saluda's Tastee Freeze.

"Can't just show up at a prison." I had to fulfill my wet blanket duties. "And we need more to work with than we've got."

"Is he going to want money?" Ev asked.

"Going to want something."

"Ever take your shirt off in public?" Gus asked me. She'd been quiet for a stretch, thinking (I decided) about dead Murray standing on the beach with his fish.

I shook my head. "I won't even wear shorts."

Gus nodded. Pleased.

"You go around with your pants off."

Ev had kind of a foresight problem, so he didn't see it coming when Gus reached over the seat back and swatted him twice with her shoe.

I drove my days for Benny. Gus did some little Jeremy duty, which left Ev and Dwight to figure out what we needed for Randy Pyle. They didn't go at it the same way. Dwight preferred technology and software, while Ev was solid on the phone, had a talent for snowing people. He was glib and persuasive and could seem to be whoever he said he was.

Dwight looped in Ev to help him keep up with his flow of pep squad stuff. Those girls had a way of getting themselves photographed dead drunk and undressed, and then, of course, they had a way as well of regretting it melodramatically. It's hard to pass yourself off as chaste and pure after a couple of guys you caroused with shucked you down to your underthings, wrote 'Slag' on your stomach with a Sharpie, and then posted a snapshot online. You needed a techie genius to engineer redemption from that sort of thing, give people reason to believe it had never happened.

Two techie geniuses was even better, so Dwight put Ev in line for some gratitude as well, and I came home from one of my driving days and found Gus and Dwight standing in the yard. I'd parked at Benny's, chamoised his Chrysler, and then tarped it for the night before walking over to join the pair of them.

"What's up?" I asked.

"Ev's getting pep squadded," Gus told me.

Dwight nodded. "Five minutes tops," he said. "Cindy's got, like, skills."

"Tamale night?" I asked Gus.

She shook her head. "Trying something French."

I attempted to imagine what 'something French' might be since Gus couldn't (in any standard way that mattered) cook.

The front door opened, and Cindy came out. Dirty blonde hair. Green eyes. Pep Squad kulaks in black-watch plaid. Ankle socks. Kid sneakers. I felt marginally pimpy and squeamish, especially when Cindy gave us a zesty pep squad wave and told us brightly, "Bye, y'all."

Gus called them supper savory crepes, but it was just tamales under butter.

~~~

Looking back, I can pick out the point when things turned, but I certainly didn't know it at the time. Benny and I had called on a client up around Newport News, or rather we'd tracked him to a squat there because he was on the dodge from Benny. The man had made a bulk narcotic investment with funds that Benny had fronted him and then had neglected to distribute the stuff for a profit the way he'd proposed and planned.

This was a recurring theme with Benny's clients. Some of them would pick an illicit business and then become their own best customers without all the troublesome fees. The Newport News guy — his name was Kenneth — had been in rehab six or eight times by then. Kenneth liked drugs, had bought a load of them with borrowed money, and had meant to sell them to greater tidewater after he'd had just a little taste. But the part where Kenneth liked drugs turned out to be a significant problem.

Benny had made a bet like he usually did. His game was to get paid back piecemeal so there'd be plenty of interest to cushion him and make his risk and trouble worthwhile. I doubt Benny expected Kenneth to sell enough drugs to turn a legitimate profit, but Benny had decided that Kenneth would take his payments seriously, that he had enough respect for and fear of Benny to keep current and on schedule no matter how shiftless and no count he was.

So Benny was disappointed, and disappointment had a way of making Benny irate. He preferred to be only irritated when dealing with a delinquent client since there's a fair bit of homicide potential in a dogwood staff. So once we'd located Kenneth's place out in Newport News, Benny decided we ought to have lunch first so he could calm himself a bit.

We stopped at a bistro near Christopher Newport U, and I ordered takeout for me and Benny. I was making porridge of his egg salad sandwich in the Mariner's Museum parking lot when Benny asked me how exactly the dead girl case was going.

"Funny thing," I told him. "Marco kind of showed up."

I explained about Randy Pyle and Marco's history with him.

"This come from Colby?"

I shook my head and told Benny a bit about Dwight and Ev. I was like a proud papa and (finally) a decent detective all rolled into one bundle. There I'd been a middling to sorry cop for going on an entire career and the father of a daughter her mother had never let me get to know, and now I was having an accidental family experience, which (looking back) both pleased and distracted me some.

"Pyle, you say?"

I nodded. "Used to work near where Abigail Tucker got dumped. I'm planning on having a word."

Benny ate, made his usual mess on his lunch towel, and kept dropping his flexi straw. "Buddy of Marco's, you say?"

I nodded. "I haven't talked to him about it yet. Long time ago. Druggy shit, I imagine. Sounds like Pyle never gave it up. He's locked up in Coffeewood. Don't know how he made park ranger."

"Probably friends where he needed them," Benny said. That was his steady view of the world. There was never any call for a pedigree if you were acquainted with the right people.

It all felt regular and ordinary in the moment. I wiped lunch off of Benny, and we moved on from Marco and Pyle. Back in the car, Benny got philosophical about Kenneth and his ilk.

"Nothing really takes with these people," he said. "Everything's temporary. They hate they've done whatever you're beating them for but only because you're beating them for it. I'll be needing Orlando," Benny told me, so that's the Handel I put in, and he scanned his Wall Street Journal while I drove us to Kenneth's apartment.

Kenneth's ex-wife's sister's apartment, in fact, and it turned out she had precious little use for Kenneth. He'd threatened her in his way and had shoved her around. She worked two jobs and took night classes and wasn't keen to put up with the man, especially once his druggy friends started coming over and eating all her stuff.

So she got word to Marco through her sister, and Marco passed it on to Benny, and that's how we came to be slipping up on that complex from the rear. It was the usual buckled T-11 siding and feeble trailer windows, overflowing dumpsters and tossed furniture that looked about eighth-hand. The landscaping was primarily red clay and failing shrubbery, and there were tireless bicycles chained her and there.

Kenneth had left the door standing open, probably couldn't be bothered to shut it.

I entered first and spied him at the refrigerator, parked before it studying the contents like you do. He didn't notice me, was checking what was under all the foil, so I got back to where I could block him from ducking back along the hallway. Then Benny came inside and closed the door.

"Kenneth," he said.

Kenneth raised up and left the fridge standing open. "What?" He stepped out of the galley kitchen and finally caught sight of Benny. He said what virtually all of them say. "I was just coming to see you."

"Kenneth." It was Benny's more-in-sadness-than-anger thing.

Kenneth glanced over and found me clotting up the hall. "I'm getting it tonight," he said to Benny. "All of it. Sold the whole package."

"KenNITH."

"I got double crossed, man. They robbed me, Benny."

Benny gestured with his dogwood staff for Kenneth to draw close. Kenneth did a bit and then retreated, got gestured at and closed some more.

"Honesty is the first chapter in the book of wisdom."

I got a dire twinge hearing that from Benny. He hardly ever broke out the Thomas Jefferson unless he was in a mood.

Kenneth didn't know what he was in for. "I hear you. That's saying something."

Benny smiled. I knew to look away as he landed that first blow. It was usually the worst one because it was meant to stun and disorient, and after that Benny could afford to be not merciful exactly but at least more deliberate.

Kenneth staggered and caught himself on the passthrough window between the front room and the kitchen.

"Benny, don't," he said.

Kenneth was bleeding already. Benny had caught him just above the ear, so Kenneth had a hand raised to staunch the blood and massage the sting away which left a kidney exposed for Benny to smack which, naturally, he did. Kenneth groaned and crumpled to the floor, and Benny clubbed the man again.

"Can't have this," Benny told him. "Won't do at all."

Kenneth was blubbering by then, which is common with Benny's victims. They're mostly prickly, ill-humored sorts to start with, but Benny's got a gift for draining starch.

Kenneth made a moist plea, sounded like a collie talking until Benny poked him with his staff to shut him up.

"Why am I here?" Benny asked. He had a taste for things Socratic.

"I'm late, man," Kenneth managed to tell him.

"Yes." Benny tapped Kenneth. "You're late."

Benny's ex-wife's sister came home just then with a couple of sacks of groceries. She sized up the situation, said, "Oh," and stepped back outside.

Benny jerked his head my way to have me follow her for a consult. She already had a cigarette going on the landing by the time I arrived.

"Won't kill him will he?"

"No money in that."

"He won't never have it." She took a long, determined draw. "Kenneth's . . . ." — she searched for just the right word and found it presently — ". . . trash."

"We'll get him out of here for you." That was the deal.

She nodded. "The guy my sister's with now . . ." She dropped her butt and ground it to smithereens. "Worse."

Isn't that the way. The parasites just kind of replace each other, and it was almost certain that Kenneth would knock some old lady on the head. He wasn't the type to prey on anybody with an ounce of moxie, so he was sure to find some frail grandmother with a window he could pry up. He wouldn't mean to kill her, but Kenneth wasn't the type to take much care. He'd be high and frantic and convince himself the old girl was just sleep.

But Benny would get paid off, and that, for him, was all that mattered.

I never went back inside and so can't say exactly what shape Kenneth ended up in. Benny presently came out wiping his staff with a dishtowel. That stick was oiled, not varnished, so there was the chance it would stain without the proper attention. That was Benny's thinking anyhow, though I'm inclined to doubt the danger since dogwood is about as dense as steel and hurts like hell. I know that now. The stuff is effectively nature's rebar.

Benny stayed fully detached from violence, psychologically speaking. There must be a diagnosis for that. He could shatter a cranium, lay bone bare, leave a delinquent client in a spreading pool of blood, and then wipe his stick and go on about his business.

"So," Benny said to me back in the Chrysler, "Coffeewood?"

I nodded. "If Pyle'll see us. Orlando?" I asked him.

Benny nodded and picked up his WSJ. "Si, con tutti i mezzi," he said.

ii

Ev was a natural romantic, as it turned out, given to lovesickness and pining. He felt like he'd made a connection with pep squad Cindy that they needed to pursue. Unfortunately, Cindy was almost certainly was not a romantic. She was far too cute and popular to get harnessed to even a regular walking boy and so hardly impressed as the type of girl likely to pine for a snark bucket in a wheelchair.

Dwight explained all that to Ev by saying, "Forget it."

Then Gus stepped in. "Try going slow," she told Ev. "Don't want to scare her off."

The strange thing was she meant it, believe Ev actually had a chance. Gus saw something special in him, maybe the young man little Jeremy would never grow up to be. I don't mean wheelchair-bound and acidic but instinctively decent where it came to people, the sort of guy who thought getting serviced by a pep squad girl bordered some way on wrong.

It was different with Dwight. He was happy to have what they gave him. A bit of hacking, a bit of loving up. That was the world in balance for him.

Ev wasn't built that way, maybe because he was a few years older or maybe because he'd learned more in his chair than Dwight had yet upright. Either way, Gus believed in Ev's chance and directed me to take Dwight elsewhere while they talked.

We ended up in the yard at the jungle gym.

"You guys getting along?" I asked him. "You and Ev?"

Dwight tried to make do with a nod. Dwight would always try to make do with a nod unless you didn't let him. I poked him with my finger, which earned me an "I guess."

I waited.

"He's not, like, happy, you know?"

"Got cause, wouldn't you say?"

Another nod.

"How's your mom with all this?"

Dwight snorted. "She's all Match dot commed and stuff."

"He can stay over here for a while if you want."

That wasn't what Dwight was after. "That girl, Cindy." He made a glum face and shook his head. "He's way too good for her."

Ev was back to himself by the following
morning. Life looked better. The sun was out, and
we were all making a road trip together, driving
up to Coffeewood for a chat with Ranger Randy.
Then it was family dinner night, and I was
cooking stroganoff. The Russian/Kraft American
kind; there'd be nothing French about it, so no
tamales and no butter sauce.

Our Randy Pyle interview, naturally, was built
on interlocking lies about his undoubted
innocence, a fictional witness we'd found, and the
prospect of a sizable federal judgment for
restitution. That was the kicker. We'd let Pyle
know it was likely we'd be bringing partial
payment, which was why he'd decided to see us in
the end.

The plan was for me and Ev to go in as a
crusader lawyer and his assistant, so I'd worn my
best suit (which was street-legal shabby), and
we'd dressed Ev up in some clothes Dwight's dad
had left in a trunk in their basement, a dinner
jacket and tuxedo pants that smelled of
naphthalene.

We stopped at Chancellorsville on the way out,
just west of Fredericksburg, because Dwight had
told his teacher it was a Civil War history
excursion, which meant he needed to pick up
some pamphlets and snap pictures of canons in a

field along with the Ellwood family cemetery where they'd buried Stonewall Jackson's arm.

"That ought to do it," Dwight announced. There wasn't a soul there but us. Ev wouldn't even get out of the car because he was down on the Civil War.

"Got dragged to Gettysburg once. Rained all day. Had to eat pancakes for supper." Then he allowed us to consider in silence the enormity of it all.

Coffewood Correctional was in the middle of nowhere between Culpeper and Orange. It looked like a community college campus but with hurricane fencing and razor wire. A dozen low buildings spread out in a field, all connected by cement sidewalks, and they had a couple of ball fields and basketball courts that were getting heavy use.

Randy Pyle had only been at Coffewood about two months. He was getting evaluated to find out where he ought to serve his term, and his record showed he hadn't helped himself by quarreling with the guards.

We had a file crammed full of evidentiary photos that I was supposed to drop so Ranger Randy could see them scatter — two dead girls, two daisy rings, young Marco, stuff like that. It was bordering on a plan.

We left Gus and Dwight out in the lot, and I rolled Ev up to the main gate.

The first guy had us on his clipboard and sent us on into reception, a sunny spot in a prefab building with plastic orange chairs like you'd sit in to wait for your guidance counselor.

I gave our names to a uniformed woman up front who seemed to be in charge. She checked her clipboard and said, "Oh." Then she begged a moment's leave and ducked into an office along the back wall. A guy in dress whites with stripes and epaulets came into the main room to meet us, a corporal or an admiral or something. Clearly the officer in charge.

"You family?" he asked.

I shook my head. "Legal."

"Hell of a thing. Mr. Pyle is no longer with us."

"Where'd he go?" Ev wanted to know.

The admiral had a sympathetic smile for the weirdly dressed young disabled man. He pointed at the vaulted ceiling. Ev looked up, and I did too.

"Suicide," the guy said. "This morning."

"Randy Pyle?"

He nodded my way. "We're still trying to work out what happened."

"He's dead?"

Another nod. "Hanged." He thought better of it. "Hung?"

"How? Why?"

"Cord from somewhere," he said. "We have a process."

That didn't really tell us anything worth knowing. It was like saying, "We have a spleen."

"Where exactly did it happen?"

"Laundry."

"Got pictures?"

"We have a process."

"Right. You loop us in maybe this all stops here."

He took my drift and retired with the desk lady for a consultation. The admiral never returned, but she came back out with three photos they'd run off a printer. Two angles on Randy half dangling, all pale and bloated, with tie-down cord around his neck. His feet were still kind of on the floor. He'd had to bend his knees to strangle, which implied tenacity, a kind of industriousness that Ranger Randy had not been known for.

Ev wasn't persuaded either.

"Suicide? Really?" he said to the woman.

"We have," she said, "a process."

Gus and Dwight, quite naturally, were surprised to see us back in the lot so soon.

"Problem?" Gus asked.

We filled them in. The twanger in my head was going off at full volume. This mess wasn't even

Columbo worthy. "I told Benny we were coming," I said.

"He have this kind of reach?" Ev asked me.

I nodded. "Every kind you can think of."

"But why?" Gus wanted to know.

That was a difficult question to answer. Benny was a bit like Cindy the pep squad girl where it came to efficiency and detachment. If he did this, it was simply because he didn't like what Randy might say.

"Are you working for our ball-gag guy?" Dwight asked me.

I shook my head. "If Benny's in it, it's got to be about money. That or Pyle hung himself like they said." A moment passed. "Hanged."

Ev glanced towards the gate house and informed Gus and Dwight, "They'll figure it out. They have a process."

My stroganoff turned out gummy but was bordering on igneous all the way through, so we all got too scorched to care about the texture or the taste.

~~~

I was off for the day after Coffeewood but happened to catch sight of Benny and Marco as they were coming home for the evening and Marco was parking the New Yorker. I was walking on the street like I did sometimes, mostly for the distraction and the air.

That's how I'd met Dwight. His mom was considerably less on the pull back then and would arrive home from work in a mood that Dwight had been informed was hormones doing to a woman that volcanic thing that hormones sometimes did. That's what a pep squad girl had told him anyway, and the very first evening we chatted, Dwight passed that news along to me.

He was sitting on his front stoop with his laptop. Ordinarily, I might have walked on past, but I was having computer problems, some kind of persistent crash and loop, and didn't know any children to call on for a fix.

Something broke inside the house. A woman muttered. I didn't know Belia either at the time. She was just the woman who drove the Kia and paid a fraction of her notice to the road, so I was always careful to lurk hard by the curb when I saw her coming.

"Everything OK?" I asked Dwight. There was a decent amount of thumping from the house.

"Mom's throwing a wobbly," he told me.

"Did you do something?" It seemed a reasonable assumption.

"Hormones."

Belia shouted, "Dwight!"

He stood up but didn't seem to know which way he ought to go.

"My computer needs fixing. I'll pay you."

Dwight came off the front steps like I'd lassoed him and tugged.

So walking the block was nothing out of the ordinary for me, which let me make it seem normal to come across Benny and Marco closing their day. Benny had landscaping he liked to check on in the hummocky beds close by the house. Azaleas and butterfly bushes and big clumps of lilies and monkey grass.

He was inspecting some kind of thorny vine and Marco was buffing a fender as I strolled up.

"What is this?" Benny asked me. He meant the prickly vine.

"Looks kind of weedy."

"Isn't that the way." He worked at it with his dogwood staff. "Healthiest thing here."

"Pull it?" I asked him. Benny nodded, and I jerked the thing out roots and all.

"Cottonwood today?"

"Yesterday," I told him.

Benny pointed at me and said to Marco, "Went to see Randy Pyle."

Marco muttered and shook his head. "Hope you didn't lend him money."

"Couldn't," I said. "He killed himself."

I could see Marco was genuinely surprised by the news, since he wasn't remotely enough of a thespian to fake it.

Benny managed a "Hmm", which wasn't enough with him to draw a conclusion from.

"What did you boys used to get up to?" I asked Marco. Of course, I had the police reports, the booking records, knew the details already.

"All drug mess back then," Marco told me. "We'd do anything to stay high. A lot of stealing, if I remember right."

That was close, from what I'd seen.

"What did you want to see Randy for?" Marco asked.

"Didn't I tell you about his cold case?"

Marco kept buffing and shook his head. He legitimately didn't know.

"Tucker was it?" Benny asked me.

I nodded. "Abigail."

Marco looked clueless. Not trying to look clueless, but like he'd authentically never heard the name before.

"Not ringing a bell but . . . like I said, I was on the needle back then."

"You're my tomorrow, right?" Benny asked me.

I nodded.

"Got to see a woman," he told me, "way down in Southern Shores. Half hour early OK? Mags might ride along."

Back at the house, I found Gus cleaning the bathroom. She had a 'boy' problem where it came to the commode. "Aim, for Chrissakes." She said that quite a lot, but we still slopped and splashed and failed to swab in any useful way. So Gus had on her yellow latex gloves, her Clorox spray, her special sponge, and I wandered in at just the wrong moment for a creature with a penis.

She gave me a look.

Short of surgery, there was no happiness I could supply her just then.

"Boys at Dwight's?" I asked.

She nodded.

"Need to call a meeting."

"Good."

I texted. The boys came over unwarned, and I let Gus have them first. Have us really, and she made us do that thing where we all gathered in the bathroom doorway. Gus had taken the toilet seat off by then so as to better reveal the comprehensive urinary dereliction we'd committed.

She talked to us at length, but it all came down to "Aim, for Chrissakes."

We didn't just mumble and retire from the doorway. We'd learned that lesson already, so we stayed where we were until Gus had exhaled with some violence and finally told us, "Go on."

The boys chewed on me some in the command center for walking them into an ambush.

"It's not even about me. I sit down." That's what Ev always said.

"Benny," I told them. "Need all you got."

"What happened?" Ev asked.

"No sure. Just getting a feeling."

They'd been poking around on Benny for poking's sake. He kept a rather low profile for a man who committed assault in a regular way.

"Give me your impressions from what you've found," I told them. "Start at thirty-thousand feet."

Ev took the first swipe and began with Abigail Tucker — her Barrel Point people, her adopted family, her girlfriends from school, and the stray commentary that Colby and his partner had put together at the Norfolk PD. "Seems accurate," Ev said, "as far as it goes, and no Benny anywhere."

"Girl had a vodka problem," Dwight told me and located the document he needed from the board and put it in my hands. It was a statement from a Kennard neighbor, mostly ignored because it was noncommittal and full of didn't sees and I don't knows.

The boys had highlighted a detail in yellow marker — "Pick up after her all the damn time. Popov everywhere."

"Somebody had to buy it for her," Dwight said.

"Ball gag guy maybe," Ev suggested.

"Kind of a bad swap for vodka, don't you think?"

"Not if you're into it," Ev said.

I found the Polaroid on the board, unstuck it and had a fresh look. Flush freckled face. Perspiration. Headgear. Yellow ball. Eyes on the lens. No fear.

"If she was willing, what happened?" I asked them. "Why make her dead."

Those boys had a special file in a drawer I used for crap and clutter. Dwight drew the drawer open and fished it out from underneath the flashlight batteries and spent Scotch tape rolls and canceled checks and rubber bands.

They had some early Benny material printed out and stuck away, so early I hardly recognized the man in the photographs. They were surveillance pics for the most part.

"Federal?" I asked.

They both nodded.

Gus came in smelling of Lysol, had a glance. "What did y'all hack?" she said.

"Who's this?" I pointed at the guy in the photo Benny appeared to be listening to.

"Lawyer from Portsmouth," Ev told me.

Gus took the photo and had a stare.

"Who?" I asked.

Ev and Dwight both winced and waited.

"Jeremy's dad," Gus said.

"Did Benny work for him?" I asked.

"Not sure," Ev said. "His only client is some holding company. Could be Benny works for them."

"Works?"

The boys nodded.

"Urbanix Global," Gus told me as she gave the photo to Dwight. "Met the CEO once. Capped teeth. Nice shoes. Real creeper."

Dwight shoved a document my way. A police report, or notes anyway scrawled on a half-completed Norfolk form. A sexual assault complaint a cop had quit in the middle of. The girl was Kathy, last name scratched out. Her age was still visible — sixteen. There were two other names inside a deep doodled pen-mark border. One was Laird Peltier. The other, Randal Pyle.

"Laird Peltier? That's a real name?" I asked.

"Big cheese," Gus told me. "Caps and shoes."

"Randy Pyle worked for him," Dwight said.

"Doing what?"

"Security." That from Ev.

"Benny too? Security?" I asked.

"Hard to tell with him," Ev said.

"Pyle was a con," I said. "Security?"

Ev showed me Pyle's entry in the personnel file.

"Have I mentioned how much I hate a coincidence?"

The boys and Gus all nodded.

"What exactly am I supposed to do with all this?" I was asking myself more than I was asking them. "'Hey, Benny, turns out you knew that guy you said you didn't know. Remember? The dead one?'"

They all nodded like that was just the sort of thing they thought might work.

"Let's say you're making chat," Ev said. "You're driving around. You just come out and ask him stuff."

"Perfect," I told him. "Tomorrow maybe. We're going to the beach."

iii

Mags did ride along with us to Southern Shores, and she dressed up for it. Benny had promised her lunch at some swanky place in Duck. We were hitting OBX in the offseason, so it was barely more than an hour down to the Wright Memorial Bridge and then across the sound and straight to a Southern Shores house about a half mile off the ocean. It was one of those flat-roofed, cinder block places that the storms had spared for years.

I eased into the drive. The wind was screaming out of the north, and you could hear the sand hitting the side of the sedan, which was no help to Benny's mood.

"Wait right here," he told Mags and then pointed my way. "You're with me."

I followed him to a door off the back deck. It was unlatched, and we went straight into the kitchen where an ancient terrier with grubby eyes lifted his head off his nasty blanket to grumble at us. The place smelled of mentholated cigarettes and scorched grease.

The residents were having a tiff, we could hear them well enough. It sounded like the lady of the house was grinding down her mate who was getting the I-should-have-listened-to-my-mother catalog of complaints. Even out of sight, he came across as a sad sack, a bust as a breadwinner, and not the sort of man who was the least bit handy around the house. Worse still, he'd stepped out with "that bitch Donna" which the wife found mystifying because the husband had no boudoir skills and Donna was built like a pulling guard.

"Won't fit," he said. "You sure this is right?"

"You've got it upside down," she told him.

We followed their racket back to their home office. I left Benny to make the brand of entrance he preferred to make, which was sly and surreptitious like he'd materialized on the spot. I didn't join him until I'd heard the usual client noises, that breathy blend of shock and dread.

"I was just about to call you," the woman said. Her name was Betty. She had a walnut and brass plaque on her desk that said so.

Benny told her, "Right," the way he does. "What's your trouble?" Benny asked, talking to the husband now.

He was holding a printer cartridge. "Can't make it fit."

"Upside down," Betty said.

"Isn't," he insisted back. He didn't appear to have a desk or a walnut and brass name plaque himself.

Benny turned my way. "Help him out."

I figured I'd step over and take the cartridge, and Benny would whack somebody. He wasn't above striking a woman, but the husband was easier to reach, so I closed on the man, took the printer cartridge from him, and moved on to the printer where I slipped it right in once I'd flipped it around because it was upside down.

Nothing happened behind me beyond what I'll have to call an exhortation. Benny encouraged Betty to get current with him and even gave the woman a week. It was enough to make me wonder if she was blood kin, maybe a sister. Benny's usual approach to business had no slot where merciful might fit, but there he was cutting a delinquent client some dogwood-free slack, and the husband was such a ready target, almost built for a blow or two.

"Big job fell through," Betty explained, and Benny just stood there and let her. "Got another one. Sending the contract now." She had a toxic look for the mister. "Trying to anyway."

"Fixed?" Benny asked me.

"All set."

"Okay then," he told Betty mostly. "We'll leave you to it."

I decided he was lulling them and would there at the end wheel around and give the mister a stout knock on the noggin, and he'd send up the usual showy geyser of blood. It didn't happen though. I followed Benny through the kitchen, past the grumpy terrier, and out into the gritty north wind.

"That sure was . . . understanding," I said.

"Like to mix it up," Benny told me just as we reached the Chrysler.

I opened his door for him and shut it behind him. I'd been with Benny for a couple of years by then, and I'd never seen him mix it up once.

I drove Benny and Mags a few miles up the road to Duck where they took lunch at a resort, one of those places built to look like a sprawling plantation by the sea. I got left on my own and found a little bookshop on the sound side in a shopping plaza.

I checked in with Gus, like I did sometimes, and she sounded surprised to hear from me and slightly irritated, which reminded me why I didn't bother to check in all that often.

"How's the beach?" she asked.

"Windy. Cold. A lot of sand down here."

"I've heard."

"How's the command center?"

"Quiet. Dwight's at school. Ev's surfing porn."

"Am not," I heard him shout.

"You want something?" she asked, like I wasn't much use to her away from the stove or out of the coat closet.

"Weird thing," I said. "Came all this way, and Benny didn't hit anybody."

"Day's young."

She was little short of prophetic. Benny and Mags had a two-hour lunch, and then Benny had me drive down to Kitty Hawk to a spot where I could park and we could walk out on the beach.

There was a sandy strip between the dunes, and Benny had some trouble with it. It was challenge enough for Benny to walk on solid, level ground, so I helped steer him by an elbow while Mags, for her part, ran ahead of us and down onto the beach. The tide was out, and she went searching a shell bed while me and Benny only made it so far as the spine of the dunes.

"This'll do," he told me.

There was nobody but us around. The sea was rough, and the gusts were stinging. I figured Benny might need his coat, and I was about to offer to fetch it when things got interrupted by a blow to the side of my head.

I didn't quite know what had happened because I didn't feel pain exactly. I was stunned and momentarily blinded, didn't decide to but just sat. Another blow followed — small of my back. I'd seen scores of people on the business end of Benny's dogwood staff, and most of them did what I ended up doing by way defense and self-preservation, which was nothing. Not a blessed thing at all. I couldn't even get organized enough to raise an arm.

I believe I said, "Hey!" but I'm not sure of that.

I was bleeding, of course. I could feel it warm on my ear. Benny handed me his handkerchief and pointed to where I should press it.

"Past is prologue, sport," he told me.

I squinted up at him. The first blow had knocked my left eye out of focus, and the right one was too watery for me to see anything much.

"Why start with this sort of stuff now?"

I felt like I knew what he meant. I'd been a slouchy, unambitious cop, had done my twenty and gotten out, and suddenly I'd decided the time was ripe to be industrious and dogged.

Mags waved from the beach and Benny waved back. "Why did you make me do this?" Benny asked.

The shock was wearing off, and my head had begun to throb. I checked Benny's handkerchief. It was soaked through.

"Here," Benny said and stuck the knobby end of his staff down where I could grab it and steady myself as I climbed onto my feet.

Benny glanced at the side of my head. "Always looks worse than it is."

Mags drove back to Suffolk, and she was about half full of champagne, so the trip was more interesting than Benny would have liked. He was up front trying to keep her between the ditches while I wallowed around in the back seat, bleeding a little still, hurting a lot.

Dwight was in the kitchen when I came in through the back door and clued me into the general impression I made by gaping at me and telling me, "Christ!"

Gus doctored on me with an overabundance of peroxide and not terribly much tenderness. I sat on the edge of the bathtub for it, and they were all in there with me.

"What do you think?" Gus asked the boys. "Stitches?"

Dwight was too squeamish to look close. Not Ev. "I'd pull that piece off and fold that one."

"Stitches are good," I said, but I didn't get a vote. Gus pulled and folded and taped me down. She kept sopping me with peroxide.

"Who do you think he's heard from?" Gus asked.

"Maybe your daddy-in-law," I told her.

My crew had been busy while I was visiting the beach. They'd worked up all the Urbanix Global principals they could find. The guy with the caps and the shoes who Gus had met and a bunch of well-heeled underlings, including big Jeremy's father who looked like a central casting aristocrat.

"Why don't we go see him?" Ev suggested all bubbly and excited.

I pointed at my parted scalp and told him, "Reason."

"He's just one guy with a stick," Gus told me. "You can always hit him back."

Gus clipped a part of me off with scissors, a flap of skin she'd decided I had no use for. She showed it to Dwight who had to steady himself on the towel rod.

~ ~ ~

I was just three days removed from my whack on the head when Leonard summoned me out swampside. He called my cell and simply breathed for about a quarter minute.

"Hello," I kept saying. I could hear him. He had that labored, moist, deviated septum thing going, but he only gave me breath alone and wouldn't talk.

I dropped the call. He dialed right back. His phone was from 540.

"Who is this? What do you want?"

More breathing. "Want you. Right here. Today'll work." And that was all he gave me to go on.

Gus was checking my head wound at the time, which meant more peroxide for me. I had a patch of hair above my ear that was so blonde it was sort of green.

"Who's that?" she asked.

"Remember Leonard?"

"Swamp thing?"

I nodded. "We're buds now."

Gus dabbed me with a cotton ball. "Well, you're just into all sorts of stuff."

Diego was out there. Juan might have been there too, but the guy sitting on the sofa in his undershorts and socks smacked himself on the chest and told me, "Diego," by way of putting confusion to rout.

Leonard came up from the back of the house. "What are you driving?" he wanted to know.

I followed him to the front door, which still didn't shut completely, and we looked out at my gray Biscayne, about as close to invisible as you can get with internal combustion technology.

"Got gas?"

I nodded.

Leonard turned to Diego. "Wheels are here, Boo."

Diego grunted and pulled what looked like a Mauser from between the sofa cushions.

"What happened to you?" Leonard asked as he studied the scabby side of my head.

"Walked into a tree."

"Dogwood?"

Leonard crowded close, stuck his nasty tongue out and licked my wound. He'd started and stopped before I could even spasm and be disgusted.

They had me drive them clear to Virginia Beach, and it took a while to get there. The beltway was clotted and lanes were closed on the four-lane to the coast, so me and Leonard and Diego got to spend a chunk of quality time together.

Diego sat in the back and did quite a lot of the sort of picking and scratching our primate brethren get up to on cable wildlife shows. Leonard, for his part, talked to me at length with his quoting finger raised.

"The doer alone learneth," he told me somewhere around Chesapeake. I got "In the rich man's house there is nowhere to spit but his face" near Mt. Trashmore and "Liberty consists of doing what one desires" when we were coming down off the highway at Pacific Avenue. Leonard didn't seem to wish for or expect comment back, so I was content enough just to drive. Better to get talked at than licked.

I didn't ask where we were going or why, and Leonard failed to inquire about Benny. We seemed to both understand if I knew something pertinent, I'd volunteer it, and until then Leonard would make whatever use of me he saw fit.

We stopped at three high-rise condo buildings before Leonard felt sure we'd found the right one. In his defense, they all did sort of look alike. Leonard sent Deigo into the lobby of the third one.

Diego came out nodding. Leonard opened his door and told me, "Ten minutes tops."

I eased into a spot and thought I'd sit and wait for them to return, but my newfound detective industriousness took hold and soon enough I was in the lobby talking to a guy and a girl at the desk.

I gave them my best Diego description. "Who was he looking for?" I'd been on the badge plenty long enough to know precisely what tone to hit, the one that suggests you're only being civil as long as you have to be.

The guy gave first, the way guys will. "Miranda?" he asked his colleague.

She nodded. "1406," she told me.

"He say why?"

They both shook their heads. I hung for a moment in the lobby and wasn't going up until I did. About the only thing those places offer is a view of the Atlantic. Otherwise, they tend to be dreary stacks of boxy condos with a gym on top. This one was no different, had a kind of motel hallway with over-bright lighting and hanging pots of plastic ivy for decor.

1406 was at the far end of the hall, and I couldn't afford to get caught lurking, so I was reluctant to ease down but did it anyway, stayed just long enough to hear voices from inside then the kind of thump you raise when you bounce a woman off a wall.

I couldn't decide what to do, had to be mindful of Diego's Mauser, so I just stayed long enough for voices to take over and the thumping to die away, which let me tell myself that things were fine, which let me head back to my Chevy. I was

behind the wheel looking normal by the time
Leonard and Diego came out.

"All good?" I asked them.

Diego grunted. Leonard raised his quoting
finger and told me, "The only thing I know is that
I know nothing." I didn't get an additional peep
out of him the entire trip home.

Of course, I drove all the way back to the beach
to see if the woman was dead. That captured
what life had come for me. Devil on one shoulder,
ratty angel on the other.

I rode the elevator up to fourteen and walked to
the end of the hall. I put my ear to the door
before I knocked. Nobody answered at first, but I
kept on knocking until she finally drew the door
open with the night chain on.

Miranda looked maybe thirty-five. She was
wearing a nappy bathrobe and had splotches on
her neck. When she shifted her hair with her
right hand, I could see that her wrist was bruised.

"Leonard do that?"

It was like she gave up, unlatched the chain and
retired, left me to enter if I would.

Hers was a nice place, tasteful for a Virginia
Beach condo. Spare. Hardwood instead of carpet.
Framed art photography on the walls. She was
waiting for me in the main room with a rocks
glass half full of scotch.

"What do you want?" she asked.

That was difficult question to answer. I hardly knew where to start, or if I should start at all.

"I drove Leonard over. Diego."

"They forget something?"

I shook my head. "You work for Benny?"

I could tell she didn't know the name. I still had nose enough for that.

"What do you want?"

"Heard them in here. Got kind of worried about you."

That prompted some vinegary laughter.

"You Urbanix Global?"

It was a flyer, plain and simple, but it sure got a rise out of her. She stiffened. She smiled.

"Let me show you something," she said.

Her handbag was sitting on the floor, and she picked it up and sifted through it, found what she wanted, a yellow thing that looked sort of like a pistol. She pointed it my way without hesitation and hit me with both darts.

It was dark by the time I woke up in my car. I was even buckled in, thanks (I decided) to the helpful staff.

I remembered what had happened and knew exactly where I was. I started my Biscayne and sat for about ten minutes until I felt steady enough to drive. Since Leonard wasn't available to raise a finger and quote at me, I had a go myself. St. Augustine somehow came to mind.

"'We are too weak,'" I said aloud, "'to discover the truth by reason alone.'"

Pocahontas Pancake House

i

The boys wanted to be in on the daddy-in-law thing, but Gus knew the man well enough to prevent it. I got to go as her sponsor.

"I'm making amends," she explained.

"Whiskey?"

"Pills," she said. "He'll believe it."

When I asked for some background on him, a personal impression from Gus, she gave the matter a bit of thought. "He's like his wife, but worse."

You wouldn't have known it to look at him. The boys had pulled stuff off the web, and in every photo Jeremy senior (biggest Jeremy, I liked to call him) looked like a man who'd just wandered off his yacht. Thick silver hair. Bright, blue eyes. Enough eyebrows for a throw rug. More sculpted than jowly. A fine set of choppers, and a square, noble chin. Big Jeremy, his son, was clearly the degraded version. His dad had the aristocratic stuff in its pure form.

"Who are you?" Gus asked me on the way. We were meeting in the lunch place at the bottom of biggest Jeremy's building.

"Bob Raymond. Retired salesman. Dental supplies."

"That's dull enough." Gus was driving.

"Wife left me. We raised Schnauzers."

"All right, Bob. Don't gild it."

We arrived a quarter hour early because biggest Jeremy, Gus informed me, was prissy and constipated where it came to stuff starting on time. Business meetings. Tennis matches. Social events. Sex probably.

He had two floors of one of those old brick refits smack downtown a half a block from the MacArthur Center, and the bistro where we were meeting him sold their goods at airport prices. Four dollar coffee. Twelve dollar pimento cheese sandwich. Chips extra. Like that.

The manager of the place was just starting to give us trouble for clotting up a table and ordering nothing when daddy-in-law strolled in to join us, and the mere sight of him shut the woman up. He winked at her. She all but darted off to fetch his usual latte.

"Hello, you," he said and kissed Gus on both cheeks.

"Bob Raymond." We had one of those competitive handshakes. I lost.

"Pleasure, Robert." He claimed to be Jerry, I can't imagine even his mother called him that.

He had on a watch that surely cost more than my car and a gray suit that was shiny but in that tasteful, elegant way usually reserved for British cinema. Shell cordovan brogues. A matching belt. Monogrammed silver cufflinks. Titanium eyeglasses. He was an awful long way from Jerry, more on the Your Worship end of things.

I didn't know exactly what Gus had in mind because she wasn't the sort to make a plan and tell you all about it. I'd tried to pump her on the way, of course, but she'd only said, "You'll see."

So I sat there being Bob the sponsor while Gus and biggest Jeremy caught up. It was all domestic fantasy. He spoke about his wife as if she were a normal loving human, and Gus filled J Daddy in on little Jeremy's exploits on the soccer pitch and accomplishments in school without referring at all to the T Bird he'd trashed while on a drunken spree.

Upper crusty sorts, I've noticed, are Olympic-quality ignorers. They can sort out all the bad stuff and shove it off in a slot somewhere, treat it like it doesn't exist and never actually happened while the blue collar way is to go with bald facts in their proper rank and order. Your daughter might be a slut and a meth head but she holds her job and takes decent care of her babies. I don't know that one's better than the other, but one's sure closer to the truth.

"So," biggest Jeremy said once they were all caught up, "you twelve-stepping it now?"

Gus recited a snatch of self-help dogma and nodded.

"Didn't realize it was this bad."

"I hid it, trying to keep it from J and J."

"But she's kicked it?"

That was for me. "On her way," I allowed, and then I gave him the whole bit about it being a slog and a struggle. I had more of that sort of palaver, but he waved me off and turned away.

"I forgive you," he told Gus, "if that's what you're here for."

"Thanks." She laid a hand to his arm as she spoke.

He was ready to go. Nobody needs terribly much of an in-law.

"Laird Peltier," Gus said before he could stand. "I need to pay him a visit as well."

"Why?" Biggest Jeremy was a notch or two more interested now — maybe just that lawyerly thing, instinctively looking out for a client.

"We have kind of a . . . history." Gus winced and looked persuasively embarrassed.

"You and Laird?"

"Me and Laird and Darvocet."

"When was this?"

Gus shrugged. "Some party. I sort of threw myself at him."

"At Laird?" Boy did he sound unpersuaded like this was not a possibility.

She nodded. "He was a gentleman. Walked me around. Had his driver take me home. I just need to acknowledge it and seek his forgiveness, apologize to the man, face to face," Gus said.

"We have a process," I added.

That earned me biggest Jeremy's you-still-here? glance.

"Five minutes," Gus said.

Biggest Jeremy pointed at me as if to ask, "This dweeb coming too?"

Gus nodded.

He pulled out his phone and sent a text. He got an answer within thirty seconds. "They'll squeeze you in," he told Gus. "Talk to Evie. They're on Brambleton."

He stood. More kissing. Another longshoreman's handshake for me. Then he was gone in his air of elegance just as the manager showed up with his latte.

"So?" Gus asked me.

"Nice watch," I said, "and Laird Peltier might be gay."

"I kind of got that too. Go get squeezed in?"

It should have been about a two-minute ride, but we got lost in downtown Norfolk where they can never quite settle on which direction their one-way streets should go. We ended up parking in a dreary cement garage, two levels underground with pigeons in it.

"What are you thinking?" I asked Gus on the elevator ride up.

She told me (like I knew she would), "You'll see."

Urbanix Global had elegant offices, teak accents wherever wood could go and rubbed brass everywhere else. Gus gave our names to the woman at reception, and then Evie came out to get us.

We followed her and waited a little while longer in Laird Peltier's outer office. Evie got dinged, and we got sent into the big chief's presence. More teak. More brass. No paperwork in sight. A desk the size of a double bed, and a splendid view of the Elizabeth River.

Laird Peltier looked like he had to. Sixty trying to pass for forty, and he'd sought and received more help than most men ever would. Implants and plugs and peels and injections. He gave the impression of a man who wasn't entirely real. Beautiful bespoke shoes, though, on his tiny, narrow feet and perfectly manufactured teeth the shade of institutional porcelain.

Gus made the introductions, and Laird Peltier clearly had no idea who she was.

I could see it in his eyes. He showed Gus his dazzling choppers and nodded while Gus gave him a full accounting of just how badly she'd behaved.

"Big place on the beach, remember?"

He didn't

"Brought both my sisters with me."

That's when my brain told me, "Uh oh."

Laird Peltier was still nodding and smiling. "Yes, charming." The man was merely being polite.

"I've got pictures," she said. "I'm so proud of them." She dug in her purse and pulled out a single sheet of folded printer paper. Abigail Tucker and Julie Fay Greer were on it —not as corpses, thankfully, but both in life.

Laird Peltier did the polite thing and took what Gus offered and gave the two girls what started as a casual look. He opened his mouth like he intended to tell Gus something frothy and pleasant, but then something clicked in his head, and he seemed to realize who he was looking at. He didn't make any kind of racket. It was in his eyes alone and didn't last. He recovered and went back to normal since you don't get to be top dog at a place like Urbanix Global by giving much of anything away.

"Pretty girls," he said. "Can't place them. Are you entirely sure it was me?"

"Thought it was," Gus told him. "Hope it was." She glanced at me and laughed. "Can I apologize to him anyway?" she asked.

I nodded. "We have a process."

"Do it," Laird Peltier told her and smiled. He was entirely himself again.

Gus went through what sounded like a drug rehab catechism. "Ok?" she asked me once she'd finished.

"We're good," I said.

I knew we weren't and told Gus as much once we were in the elevator. "He knew who they were. You see it?"

Gus nodded.

I followed her off the elevator and into the parking garage. She had some kind of shoe trouble and leaned against a car to fix it. A dirty, white Buick Regal, and that's where they tracked us down. One musclebound no-neck, one wiry shiftless looking guy with Prince Valiant hair.

They were wearing matching blue sports coats and gray slacks. Urbanix Global security goons, I had to figure. There was no running away from them, so we just stayed where we were.

"Gentlemen," I said.

The big one swiped the air and the baton in his hand telescoped and clacked. As he stepped towards us, I grabbed and sheltered Gus and waited for the sting of the thing, but he went for the Buick rear window instead. It took him two blows to break it. Then it was on to the passenger side glass, and he busted all that as well. The windshield followed. The driver's side glass. Even both rearview mirrors. If you're going to have musclebound no-neck on staff, you'd want a thorough one like him.

Then he collapsed his baton against his thigh, and his partner stepped in. It's hard to take a man seriously who hooks his hair behind his ears.

He got close, too close, and told us in a raspy whisper, "Careful."

Then they retired in their homely politburo outfits back into the gloom of the garage.

I thought I might have to comfort Gus, but she wasn't so easily rattled. Gus brushed glass off the trunk lid and asked me, "Should we leave a note?"

~~~

The trouble with crime as a general rule is that guilt's a complicated thing. There's Jean Valjean on one end and most everybody else on the other because circumstances and poor luck can often conspire to make something ghastly happen, and the people can get snared in covering it up. Sure there are monsters roaming, but they're specialists and rare.

"I doubt," I told the boys, "Laird Peltier's interested enough in girls to kill two, especially not by accident and seven or eight years apart."

Gus nodded by way of confirmation and so disappointed them further.

"We've got to figure out who's in this exactly and why," I said. "Benny? Ranger Randy? Marco? Leonard? The Guatemalan boys?."

"Something's going on," Ev told me, "or why bust up a car?"

We were all in agreement. Something was going on. After all the time and effort invested, that was not a lot to have.

"What do we need?" Dwight asked.

"What have you got?"

"Some new Benny stuff," Ev told me. "Excel spreadsheet."

Ev pulled up a ledger page on his laptop screen. It made no sense to me, a lot of sums strung out in columns.

"That guy's rolling in it." Ev pointed out several lines of figures. "Money coming in from everywhere, including here." He tapped the screen. Just above his finger was the word 'Urbanix'.

"Twenty K a month," Dwight told me, "and he's not in any of the paperwork. The principal investors, the board, employees, like that."

"He's in this," Dwight said. "Got to be."

I made my noncommittal necknoise. "Only if they owed him money."

Ev grumbled and told me, "Might hit you in the head with a stick myself."

I knew how they felt. I'd been where they were back when I was just out of uniform and the green guy in the squad room. I'd been eager there at first to make things happen fast. We'd go out on cases, and I'd draw my conclusions for all the usual reasons. Wives disappeared when their husband's helped them, and friends could come to fatal blows over not terribly much at all. Proximity mattered quite a lot. Money too. Frequently Wild Turkey and Old Crow.

They had started me with an old guy who dragged around and complained about his hip. Buzzy, they all called him, and he looked to be hanging on for his benefits, or that's what I'd concluded before I knew any better because concluding was what I did the most of back then.

Buzzy had his blind spots, and he wasn't above taking favors, but there was still plenty of stuff going that Buzzy believed somebody should do time for, so he could put a case together when that sort of thing was needed, and he always went in unconvinced of exactly what he thought. That sounds easy enough and sensible, but it isn't natural at all. We look at the facts and pick our villains, so it's kind of a chore to stay neutral and wait.

Buzzy didn't actively instruct me, never sat me down for pointers but instead just let me be wrong for about a half a year. Decisive and off base was my fortè, but I was slow to recognize it until a dead woman at a motel — a Saudi national in the bath tub — tempted me to go wrong all over the place while Buzzy just waited around. She had a husband and a lover (who had a husband too), and a son who was down on lesbians in a vitriolic way. There was motive to spare and opportunity aplenty, so I did my thing and ranked my villains while Buzzy took notice of the fresh lithium grease in the door lock, studied up on the motel occupants, and then arrested a guest downstairs.

He hadn't known the woman. He'd seen her check in. Fine luggage. Pricey clothes. And he'd gone up thinking she was out. They'd surprised each other — her drawing a tub and him on a pilfer. Holding her under had seemed at that moment the thing he ought to do.

I still sort of liked the girlfriend's son even after the confession, but that's when Buzzy finally counseled me. "Don't be a schmuck," he said.

"Benny's not my friend," I told those boys. "He pays me to drive him. That's all. Could be, he's up to the armpits in this. Off what you've got, I'm saying don't decide."

At that very moment, my cellphone range. I checked the screen — Benny calling. You didn't not take a call from Benny.

"Gentleman's club in thirty?" he asked.

"Drive you?"

"I'm already here."

I got handed my gun again by Gus. "Couldn't find a helmet," she said.

Ev chimed in as well, of course. "Hope not deciding's enough."

Benny had killed one man I knew of. I couldn't figure Marco would lie about such a thing, and it sounded precisely like the sort of flogging Benny would get up to with the wild card being that the fellow he was beating had a coronary problem, so he proved to be a poor candidate for getting knocked around.

"Seized up." That's what Marco told me. "We put him in a bin somewhere."

I hadn't been in the club since cousin Dennis' management had truly known the time to take hold. He'd routed the pretensions and blue-collared the place up pretty good, so now it was clearly just a strip joint with a pile of flesh named Hog Man at the door. That was what the tattoo on his right forearm said anyway. He had an index finger like a dowel rod and poked me with it as I tried to go inside.

"Five damn dollars."

I'd never paid for a beating before, particularly one that would possibly lead to a coronary and a bin.

Inside was cluttered and junky and underlit so you couldn't see much of the other patrons but mostly just the girls where the scarlet spotlights played. I didn't recognize any of them. It looked like Dennis had turned the strippers over for a shabbier, cheaper variety of creature. They didn't dance so much as skulk around and litter the stage with clothing. The PA was so poor, it sounded like they were all named Brandy. Two were always up on the poles at once doing halting, ungainly things.

From what I could see, the joint was half full, and the patrons were mostly crowded around the stage with their tongues sticking out, pipe fitters and framers on late lunch break, a few dock workers mixed in.

Dennis saw me before I saw him and shouted out from the bar.

"Looking good," I hollered to make myself heard to him over the Def Leppard. "Benny?"

He pointed towards the side door where the dressing rooms and the office were.

I went on in and surprised a pair of Brandys in the altogether, and I pointed at the office door by way of excusing myself. I knocked and got admitted by Marco who'd just shoved a half a slider into his mouth.

Benny was at the desk, one of those massive oak things with a hole in the clutter in case you needed some working space. Benny had a tin pie pan before him with corn dodgers in it and some mashed up breaded shrimp.

"Eat yet?" he asked me.

I was agreeably empty. Better for getting shoved around and smacked, so I told Benny, "Yes."

Benny pointed me to an empty chair. There was another one by the door, and I watched as Marco shifted it to wedge it snug under the knob.

"Keeps the girls out," Marco told me. Or the troublesome colleague in.

"I got a call." Marco removed his towel bib and wiped his fingers. "Two calls."

He paused for me to ask him who from, but I was too good at waiting for that and so just sat there and gave him all the gap he could stand.

"Friends in high places."

I waited some more.

Marco was eating French fries and so hardly looked prepared to club me. Benny's dogwood staff was leaning against the far wall and out of reach. Of course, my Ruger was under the front seat of my Biscayne, so I was no better off than them.

"What's the story?" he asked me.

So I told him. "Got a murdered girl. Two of them. First one was found up where Randy Pyle worked. We go to ask him about it, but he gets dead. We see he used to draw from Urbanix Global, go in to see the big boss there, and he sends us off with goons. I sure wasn't the best cop going, but my nose has always worked fine."

"Those kids digging all this up?" Benny asked.

I nodded. "If it can be found, they'll find it."

"Been to Colby with any of this?"

I shook my head. "Got nothing for him."

"How'd you get started with this business anyway?" Benny swabbed his face with his napkin.

"Magnolia Hills," I told him. "Out there watching my Uncle Homer die. Guy in the hall put me on it."

Benny laughed, and I could hardly blame him. He was about as big on serendipity as me.

"Who do you like?" he asked me.

I shrugged and meant it because we had nothing solid. "I'll take anything you can tell me."

"Me and him," he glanced at Marco, "we're both clean."

Then he pointed at his dogwood staff and asked me to fetch it, which I did and handed it over to him. I had faith somehow I wouldn't get brained, and Benny just wiped his stick and looked at me and then ran his fingers over the knot end in a sensuous, art-appreciation sort of way.

"How's this?" he said. "Two weeks. Finish it or drop it."

Since he didn't sound interested in a counter offer, I nodded. "Help if you could throw me a crumb."

Benny gave that some thought and obliged me. "Laird Peltier? Isn't him."

"Why the goons then?"

"Listen harder. Isn't him.

I knew it meant something but couldn't begin to figure what.

"Crumb for me?" Benny asked.

Since I had to give, I gave. "Leonard. You know, guy out by the swamp?"

Benny nodded.

"Might want to watch your back."

Benny and Marco had a moment, exchanged significant glances as if I'd cemented something they'd already half decided.

"Leonard," Benny told me by way of further reward, ". . . he's not as clean as us."

ii

So it was fourteen days and out for us, no matter where we ended up, which didn't mean we couldn't take time for Ev's twenty-third birthday party. His mom, Janet, drove down from Chincoteague and brought Ev new fingerless gloves along with a case of Yoo-Hoo he made a big show of having outgrown.

Janet had booked a motel, but Belia insisted she stay with her, and they passed a couple of nights together as single moms on the prowl. I knew better than to encourage Gus to join them, since there are women like Belia and Janet who are either with men or temporarily between them and creatures like Gus who stand apart, often without trousers. I didn't have Gus in any real sense. Clearly, big Jeremy didn't either, and he'd bought the swanky house and fathered the child and signed all the nuptial paperwork.

Janet proved to be a squeamish thing and so tolerated our command center poorly. Too many well-lit, crisply-focused photographs of corpses for her taste, but she was pleased to see Ev engage in something that at least appeared constructive.

She confided to me and Gus on the QT, "He used to just chat and stuff." I took that to mean Ev incinerated people on comments threads across the globe, and I didn't bother to tell Janet he still made time to slag people off worldwide.

"And he's got a girl?" Janet sounded hopeful bur. "Cindy?"

I let Gus take that one. She made an affirmative-ish noise and nodded.

"What's she like?"

"Pretty." Gus looked my way.

I nodded.

"Cute," Gus said, "the two of them together."

"So she's . . . real?" Janet asked.

"Very real," I told Janet. "She comes around a lot." Then I ran out of material. "Cute," I said, "the two of them together."

Cindy actually showed up in the flesh while Janet was fixing to leave. We didn't have to worry about prepping Cindy for any lies we'd told about her because she was not the brand of girl to engage necessarily in the world as it was. She had her stuff she needed, her things she wanted, and everything else was just rocks in the road that she'd meet with a sigh, a "Whatever".

Gus introduced Cindy to Janet and made it clear she was Ev's mother, and Cindy treated Janet to her usual blank look, while she mouthed a weary version of, "Hey." Then it was on to Ev who could do something for her that she currently needed done.

As Cindy kneeled beside Ev's chair, her tiny skirt got even tinier. Gus said to Janet (but for me primarily) "Cute, the two of them together."

Of course, we hadn't stopped working entirely all through the festivities, which involved a night out eating fully cooked tamales and drinking awful bar-brand tequila in lousy margarita mix, followed by a day of recovering from it — lots of tap water, some groaning. But we were all along dredging up and chewing on details independently, so once Janet had headed back north and it was just us four again, we each had more than a little to tell the others.

"All right." Gus took the emcee job. She pointed Dwight's way. "Go."

Dwight had been working on Benny's financials. It turned out Orin, Benny's number's guy, was good with sums but bad with tech, so Dwight had successfully hacked into just about everything Orin had.

"He's definitely getting a regular payment from Urbanix Global. Expense on their end. Income on his. All proper. All filed."

"Paid for what?" I asked.

I kind of knew what was coming. "Consulting," Dwight told me. That covered a dumpster full of sins. "It comes through his office." Dwight pointed at Gus.

"Jeremy senior?" she asked.

Dwight nodded.

I tried to imagine Benny giving advice that didn't involve his dogwood staff. "I don't suppose Peltier and them would need to borrow money from Benny," I said.

Dwight shook his head. "Not a chance."

"So it's some kind of payoff."

"For . . . ?" Ev asked.

"Knowing Benny . . . silence. He's good at that."

"Why don't they just goon him?" Gus wanted to know.

"Benny knows how to stay bought," I said.

"And Leonard?" Gus asked. She pointed at Ev.

He'd pulled up a fair bit of Leonard dirt and set about sharing it with us.

"Uber rat, this guy," EV cataloged Leonard's various charges and scant record of indictment. Leonard had testified for county prosecutors in four states and was listed as a witness in a federal investigation. "Drug stuff. Atlanta," Ev said.

"Think he's up to killing our girls? Was he even around for it?" I asked.

"Maybe and yep." Ev gave us dates. He'd plotted Leonard's movements as best he could. "Not much violence here," Ev said of Leonard's booking sheets. "More of a professional creep. Gets buddies to do the rough stuff for him."

"How about disposal?" Gus asked, and that got a nod from Ev.

"And he knew Randy Pyle. They were in Fairfax County holding together."

"Booked together?" I asked.

Ev nodded. "Larceny. Possession."

"So why are Leonard and whosey," Gus asked, "beating up a woman in Virginia Beach?"

Ev looked to Dwight who told us, "Miranda Knox." He pulled up more financials on his laptop screen. "Nice portfolio. No job. Eight thousand a month into her account."

"Jeremy senior?" Gus asked.

Dwight nodded. "More consulting," he said.

Dwight and Ev wouldn't wait in the parking lot, so we all went into the lobby of Miranda Knox's building where I was reunited with my brace of concierges from before. They both proved accomplished at not seeming to recall me, the guy they'd almost certainly wheeled out unconscious and put in his car.

I sure remembered them. Read their names off their tags and was chatty. "1406, right?"

"She just went out," the guy told me. He glanced sheepishly at his colleague, figuring he'd volunteered too much.

"Boardwalk probably," she the girl said as she watched Ev grab a grubby handful of taffy out of the bowl on the counter.

Offseason Virginia Beach is passable if you hit it on a dreary day. Wind. Clouds. Gulls making their screechy racket. We looked up and down the boardwalk and saw maybe eight people altogether.

I pointed. "Her."

Miranda Knox was power walking and listening to something on her earbuds. She was a couple of blocks south of us but heading up our way.

"Think she's got her zapper?" Gus asked.

I liked my odds. "Four of us, two darts."

We decided to let Ev waylay her, play the crippled boy and stop her so he could ask directions. He even made out to be a Mormon and more or less quoted some Scripture at the woman, which Miranda Knox responded to with a sigh and a sneer. He was a yutz in wheelchair; that didn't make him Billy Graham.

"What are you looking for?" she finally asked and pulled out her second ear bud.

We moved to join him as Ev said, "Looking for you."

She recognized me and gave me the weary look I'm sure I deserved.

We let Dwight start. That was the plan. "We can probably help you with Leonard?"

"Working on a scout badge?" She made a move to push past us.

"It's him or you," I told her. "How about accessory to murder?"

That proved enough to stop her.

It was Gus' turn now. "We'd be happier with him."

Gus pointed at a restaurant across Atlantic Avenue. Pocahontas Pancake House. Cheesy and convenient. Miranda Knox shrugged and relented, so we all crossed the street.

Inside, the place was a showy tribute to the Jamestown colony, with murals and headdresses, a wooden Indian, a tepee in one corner. What any of that had to do with pancakes and fried chicken, I'm sure I'll never know. Ev and Dwight ordered buckwheat stacks. The rest of us went with the usual watery coffee. We'd been seated between a totem pole and a portrait of Chief Powhatan in his war paint and feathery finery.

I made an attempt to explain to Miranda Knox precisely who I was, but she waved a hand.

"I know who you are." Then she pointed at Gus and at the boys in an inquiring way.

"We're his team," Gus said.

She looked from Gus to Ev to Dwight. The boys were inspecting the assorted syrups.

"You drive Benny," she said to me.

"I do."

"And you've got a team?"

"And we're working two murders. Go figure."

"For . . . ?"

"Shits and giggles," Gus said. "Why's Urbanix paying you?"

She did what any smart, semi-incriminated woman would do and waited for us to come up with a persuasive reason for her to tell us anything. She turned out to be good at waiting. I admired her serenity. I was working up something to say to the woman when Ev decided to chime in.

"It's Peltier's brother, isn't it? He's the bad seed."

We all shifted to look at Ev because we didn't, as a group, have that suave investigative thing down and none of the rest of us was even aware that Laird Peltier had a brother.

Ev had let his nose take him where the facts didn't entirely lead because the brother was more of a vacancy in Laird Peltier's life than a living, breathing thing. His name was Dustin, and he was five years younger with an existence that seemed to have been made up of intervals out in the world interrupted by stays in the types of institutions where rich people convalesce. Places that had names like Taunton Glen, The Idyll at Roanoke, Harrow Down.

"Troubled, right?" Ev put some spin on it. He could have meant nut job, maybe only mild depression, or some sort of raging addiction. Who could tell?

"Hard drinkers, that whole family," Dwight said to Ev. "Probably that, don't you think?"

Miranda Knox looked about equal parts gassy and amused. She was getting played by a guy in a wheelchair and his tweeny buddy.

"Why's Urbanix paying me?" she asked me and Gus primarily. "Lets me sit in a pancake house in the middle of the day."

"Accessory after the fact?" I glanced at Gus who nodded. "If it is little brother and you've been sitting on guilty knowledge, that's going all turn into lawyer money."

Looking back, I imagine Miranda Knox had been waiting for/dreading somebody like us. Well, not exactly like us.

"I don't know about any 'couple of girls'," she told us. In my mind, there's a considerable gap after, but maybe that's just me trying to goose the drama up. "I only saw one," she added.

There's not much doubt a charge went through us, all four of us at once. We'd started with a musty file, long packed away in a car shed, and had followed it to a woman who knew how Abigail Tucker had died. That's what I assumed anyway, and I gestured for Ev to dig out his snapshots, the two innocent photos we'd dug up of Abigail Tucker and Julie Fay Greer in life.

He passed them to Gus who handed Abigail to Miranda Knox. She glanced and told us, "Nope." Then Julie Fay Greer. "Uh uh."

"You sure?" I said. "The pictures might be . . ."

"She's black."

"Wrinkle." That from Ev.

"Don't know her name. Probably with catering."

"Catering?" Gus asked.

"They had a party at the aquarium."

"Urbanix?" I asked her.

She nodded. "October 2008." She toyed with her coffee cup, spun it. "Dusty was having one of his days."

It took her about a quarter hour to lay out the whole sorry business for us. Ev and Dwight worked through their flapjacks and sausage links as she spoke.

"Weird guy," she told us. "Half psychosis, half cocaine. OCD. Neurotic. Lot of bent friends."

"Is Leonard one?" I asked her.

She nodded and told us she'd walked up on Dusty by chance, was looking for stragglers because the party was over.

"He was next to the turtle thing. The case, you know? Banging that girl's head on a rock." She gave us a show of it with both hands. "Just kept at it, and he was laughing. Dusty was always laughing." She closed her eyes and took a moment. "Laird," she told us, "never laughs."

"Then what?" I asked.

"They cleaned it up."

"Who?"

"Leonard and them. They hauled her away. And I got . . . taken care of."

"What did you agree to?" Gus wanted to know.

"Never got that far. Money started coming, I knew what to do. Cops sniffed around a little, but it never went anywhere."

"Don't guess you'll tell this to a detective we know."

She stood up and dug out her ear buds. "No," she told me, "don't guess I will."

And then she left, and we just watched her. Past the carved Indian and the first Thanksgiving mural. She exchanged a hey howdy with the lady at the register and was out the door.

"Good pancakes" Ev told us all.

Dwight was right there with him. "Yeah."

~~~

So many missing black girls, more than you can even imagine. Gone from their homes and their families, from their jobs and their pets and their friends, just nowhere all of sudden, and there's not a lot of looking. Not from cops anyway, and there's only so much a flyer on a light pole can do.

The catering company had gone out of business, and the guy who'd started it had died. We made a field trip to the Virginia Beach aquarium, saw the turtles and the fake rocks and then went out back for a look at the water. The building sits on a finger of the Chesapeake called Owl Creek. There's a convenient raised walkway built out over the marshy verges.

Dwight was the one who said out loud, "Bet she went in there."

We couldn't even put a name to her, had narrowed the field to seventeen.

"Now what?" Ev asked.

The stink from the water was a tangy blend of rank and briny. I saw a beast of some sort poke its snout into the air and then sink back into the muck.

We had to wait on Leonard, nearly a week before he called me to come fetch him. He needed to go up to Richmond and pick up an "item" he called it, so I took the Biscayne swampside, and Leonard and Juan (this time) piled in. Juan was a slightly smaller version of his brother, Diego. Meaner looking and hell of a lot more sullen. He mostly chewed on his index finger and gazed forlornly out the back window like this world was an imposition on him and he'd rather be somewhere else.

We had a plan for those two, but it lacked certain details, mostly where it came to the when and how exactly. We knew where we wanted to end up, but not much else was firm.

"You'll figure it out," Gus had told me and then had turned to the boys. "He's resourceful."

I didn't much like the way she'd gotten wishful at my expense.

Leonard and Juan helped me out by assuming I was just their boy behind the wheel. We were up 460 almost to Disputanta when Juan told me, "Stop." He pointed at a BP station up ahead, and I pulled in and parked.

Juan piled out of the back and went off to pee, didn't think a thing about leaving me with Leonard who turned my way and was about to favor me with some wisdom, had raised his quoting finger and drawn a breath to speak when I struck him with my elbow flush on the bridge of the nose and then left that BP in an awful hurry.

Leonard was bleeding on everything, and I knocked onto the passenger floorboard. I stomped him a couple of times and told him, "Stay there."

He had other plans until he didn't, kept trying to get up against my advice, so he was not entirely conscious by the time I got where I was heading.

They were all waiting for me up in Spotsylvania, which seemed a long way to go for showy and theatrical effect. But they wouldn't hear of a substitute spot. They'd all voted and decided, so I drove up 95 from Richmond and found them parked in the place where we'd parked before, just up from the spot in the woods where Julie Fay Greer's body was found.

Me and Dwight mostly wrangled groggy Leonard and hauled him down into the woods where Ev and Gus were waiting by the last scrap of yellow police tape. Leaves had blown back into the divot that had held that girl's remains. Leonard was a snug fit and a gory sight, all splattered and encrusted, but he fit pretty nicely into that crease of ground.

"What did you to him?" Gus asked.

"Just kept inviting him to come."

Ev squirted a stream from his water bottle to help Leonard come around. Even still, it took him a while, and Leonard spent some time shifting and moaning before he opened his eyes and got them to focus. He looked from me to Ev in his chair, to Gus, to Dwight, and back my way.

I've got to hand to Leonard. He flat refused to get rattled. Once he'd finished looking around, he hit us with some Sun Tzu. "The supreme art of war"— he had his finger up — "is to subdue the enemy without fighting."

"Yeah," I told him, "My bad on that."

Leonard grinned like he'd let it go this time.

He glanced around at the woodland setting, which appeared to mean nothing to him, so Gus located him in this world and explained where he was and why. Leonard offered no denials, volunteered no commentary. He just looked bored and kept touching his nose and coming away with blood.

"Dustin Peltier, right? You just clean up."

Leonard glanced my way but didn't offer to answer.

"How many girls altogether?" Ev asked him.

Dwight said, "We know for sure about three?"

Leonard squinted and twitched like a man who'd maybe forgotten his English, who couldn't quite figure what we were hoping to know and didn't, in truth, much care.

"Let's bash him and leave him," Ev suggested. There were rocks all around, and Ev pointed at his favorite.

Leonard, being Leonard, just chuckled. He dabbed at his nose and checked his bloody fingers again.

When he finally spoke, he said to me, "Guess you'll be burning me with Benny."

"Might not have to bother." I picked up a rock the size of a cantaloupe.

Leonard laughed again. He looked dead confident I wasn't the sort to bash in heads.

Dwight had had his driving permit for nearly a month by then, so I let him drive the whole way back. We did 95, the Richmond beltway, 460 down towards Suffolk. Dwight did everything I would have done but at probably twice the speed.

I called Detective Colby on the way. He was working a case at the Chesapeake Square Mall, and I arranged for us to swing by and have a quick word.

Colby met us in the parking outside the Tilted Kilt, a Hooters with Caledonian pretensions, where a couple of beery patrons had sliced each other up.

Colby was in a weary cop mood when I waved him over to us.

"So?" he said.

I raised my trunk lid to show him what I had, all gagged and duct-taped up like a skeevy Christmas package.

"What are you into now, Leonard?" Colby asked.

Leonard half raised his quoting finger and made some racket behind his tape.

Verre De Mer

i

We'd gathered for Colby like students at a science fair, eager to show off our goods. I'd set him up with three fingers of bourbon, and we'd put him in the desk chair so he could pivot and swivel and see everything we'd accumulated and had on display.

"Where's Leonard?" he asked, once we'd run through our business.

"Basement," I told him.

"He chatty?"

"Will be if you're buying. You know Leonard," I said to Colby. "It's all about his hide."

"Bring him up."

Me and Dwight went into the basement to fetch him. We'd allowed Leonard to get out of his clothes and wash up and make himself decent. I'd let him have a pair of pajamas I'd gotten one Christmas and never worn. They had geese on them and big orange buttons, so Leonard was a bit of a sight with two coming black eyes and jammies along with his usual oxford shoes.

We squired Leonard into the command center, and of course he started out by raising his quoting finger. "We are more often treacherous through weakness than calculation."

Colby had the look of a man who'd been philosophized at by Leonard before.

"I can't get locked up," Leonard told Colby. It didn't take the form of special pleading but came out more like a steadfast rule for life.

"Go on then. Make me some cases," Colby said.

Leonard was prepared to be obliging and proved to be a demon for details. That was part of what made Leonard such a powerful snitch. He had a head for dates and commentary, played all the roles when he told about a thing. His stuff was part fiction, probably, but studded with facts, enough of them to make the things he said persuasive, but it was the casual tone he took that tended to get to you after a while.

Leonard would toss off the ghastly specifics, the blood spilled, the brains exposed, the dismemberment for logistic's sake (how else do you get a grown man in a suitcase, after all?), and it was all so breezy that you'd lose track of your disgust and forget, now and then, to revile Leonard in the fashion he deserved.

"The boy's got serious trouble," Leonard said of Dustin Peltier in time, tapping his temple as he spoke. "Something sets him off, and he just lets go."

"Something like her?" Gus said and pointed. "Or her?"

Leonard glanced at the dead girls on our board — leathery and desiccated — and then raised his quoting finger and said, "Beware lest you lose the substance by grasping at the shadow."

"This Dustin Peltier," Colby said, "he a buddy of yours?"

"Hold on," Leonard chimed in. "Ran an oxy deal through him. Did some clean up for the boy. We're not pals."

Ev dug around and gave Colby the scant paper we had on Dustin Peltier. Our lone photo was twenty-two years old. He looked like a surf bum, all sun-streaked hair and pink, peeling skin.

"In and out of private hospitals," Ev told Colby. "No charges here, but he had a spot of bother in Guatemala." Ev pointed Colby to the appropriate paragraph.

"Ergo Juan and Diego," Leonard said and raised his quoting, but Colby and I together shook our heads.

Leonard dribbled out the sorry story at his own pace and in pretty much his own way. The nut of it was that Dustin Peltier had long known a for, chiefly, cocaine and an appetite for girls too young to consent.

"He never did much chasing," Leonard explained. "That's how it is with people like them."

"Black girl at the aquarium?" Gus asked.

Leonard squinted at Gus like he couldn't recall her. Ev gave Colby the date. It was all we had.

"Y'all probably dropped her in the creek," I told him.

"Might have missed that one," Leonard said. He got a quick one off unfingered. "To fear death is only to think ourselves wise.

Leonard turned his attention to the Polaroid of Abigail Tucker on our corkboard. Flushed skin. Yellow ball. Frank gaze. "Wild child," he said. "Had a thing for reds and blues."

Leonard leaned in to study that photo a bit more avidly than I liked.

"That gear and mess was her thing, but it wasn't like Dusty to make a fuss." Standing next to a snitch is a bit like standing next to a brush fire. After a while, you're guaranteed to stink. So we took breaks, wandered outside, any place away from Leonard who took pains to compliment Gus on the cup of tea she brought him.

"When hospitality becomes an art," Leonard said, "it loses its very soul."

We knew about three girls. He knew about four more. "All of them sweet on Dusty for his drugs."

Leonard called them "candy hounds" and said
they'd get up to anything.

He was particular about the oddest stuff.
Fingernail polish. Shampoo scent. Bottom teeth.
Especially toes. For his part, Dustin Peltier was
mostly particular about rope. Braided cotton tie-
down cord, the store brand from Ace Hardware.

"Weird guy. Always having to touch stuff in just
the right way."

Leonard carried on for a couple of hours since
he had an audience after all. He refused to let
Colby record it but promised to repeat it all on
record once his deal with the state's attorney was
properly inked.

"Don't even have my lawyer yet," Leonard said,
"and I'm wearing damn pajamas."

At the end, Leonard took pains to congratulate
us on our industriousness. "Chased it down,
didn't you?" he said mostly to the boys and went
to no little trouble to make them shake his hand.

Colby carried off a file Dwight and Ev had put
together for him, something to show to his bosses
and get the business underway. We got left with
Leonard, and I carried him home in my pajamas.

"Worried about Benny?" I asked him in the car.
"He can't be happy with you."

I got the raised finger as I pulled into Leonard's swampside drive. "I love the man that can smile in trouble."

"You're just making this shit up aren't you?"

Leonard flung open his door, straightened his pajamas, and told me, "Thomas Paine."

~~~

They were in a dire mood back at the house. I found Gus and Ev and Dwight in the kitchen doing nothing beyond regrouping from the moral grind of listening to Leonard. They seemed to be at that point you can get to with a case where you wonder why you bothered and what good you've done aside from cataloging a bunch of nasty mess that humans can get up to.

"We're not done," I said. "It's not like the cops'll ever find him."

The police effort started and ended with Dustin Peltier's connected brother. That's how power works. The commissioner personally visited the offices of Urbanix Global and spent very nearly thirty whole minutes talking to Laird Peltier through his lawyer who educated the commissioner in just how hemmed in and stifled he was.

Detective Colby chose to tell Benny about it, and Benny passed it along to me. I was back behind the wheel of the New Yorker for a couple of days while Marco made a quick trip to the DR, and we were calling on a reliably docile client up by Craney Island who had an actual dementia issue and so could legitimately forgot to pay. Benny never hit him terribly hard because he felt it would be improper.

"Why didn't Colby just call me?" I asked him.

"Can't."

"We made the case for him."

"They don't want it."

The civilian part of me was, naturally, verging on a snit, but the cop part of me knew better and just snorted. One one side was Laird Peltier with the right kind of money and, most assuredly, the right kinds of friends versus a conniving snitch and a trigger-happy ex-cop with a shabby pedigree. That wasn't much of a contest.

Worse still the brother was probably packed away somewhere in 'treatment', so he'd probably — after an ugly trial — just end up where he was.

Of course, the department didn't want the case, and moreover it seemed likely Urbanix Global might pick up the tab on a fleet of prowlers and maybe an armored SWAT wagon or two and paper everything over, make it nice. I'd long since learned that's how life works, so I was in no position to act surprised.

Benny folded his Journal as we eased into his client's drive. "That Dustin," Benny said, "he always liked the sea air. You can stay put for this," he told me and got out.

Gus and Ev and Dwight had been working up a Dustin Peltier private institution timeline. He'd started out at a place in Connecticut, which seemed to legitimately deal with addiction, and he'd run through their program twice before he'd half strangled one of the staff.

The incident had made the Danbury News-Times, though Dusty wasn't identified by name, but the date fit as well as the near fatal circumstances, which had involved a length of rope.

After that it was California where Dustin migrated from north to south before fetching up in Michigan at a Traverse City new-agey place, and then it was on to Dixie after that — Columbia, South Carolina, and Rome, Georgia.

Unfortunately, Dustin Peltier had been nowhere for the past two years, and Ev and Dwight knew how to look but couldn't find a morsel between them. They had him at the Idyll in Roanoke until November of 2012, and then he'd gone to Harrow Down in Kentucky, east of Lexington. They wouldn't say when he'd left exactly, no matter how Ev tried to ply them, but he did manage to establish that Dusty wasn't there anymore.

I'd been thinking about what Benny had told me. "How much real estate," I asked them, "does Laird own."

That was tax stuff. No challenge. Dwight pulled it all up.

"Three places, two houses and a condo."

One was a Manhattan pied-á-terre. One was Laird's swell Ghent Square home in Norfolk, and the third was house on the beach in Carova, a place called Verre de Mer.

"Where's Carova?" Gus wanted to know, so Ev pulled up a map.

It was sort of on the Outer Banks. Well, definitely but not a civilized place like Duck or Corolla and so far north you were almost in Virginia.

"Got to drive on the beach to get there," Ev told us. "No roads. Just houses and sand."

"God spot for a nut job." Gus again.

I took a look at the satellite image on Ev's laptop screen. Better than good. Pretty stinking ideal.

It didn't hurt that the crew felt like they deserved a proper outing, had more than earned a trip to somewhere other than a prison, a Civil War battlefield, or the Virginia woods. My last visit to

OBX had gone rather poorly for me, so I was less eager than the rest of them, but that wasn't about to get in their way.

Gus borrowed Big Jeremy's school-bus yellow hummer which, given the sort of lout he was, he essentially had to own, and she even rented a place for two nights up in the vicinity. The only house she could get on short notice in the shoulder season had six bedrooms and readily slept eighteen.

It's a heck of a stupid route you have to take from Suffolk to get to Carova. All the way down to Harbinger, an hour into North Carolina, and then across the sound on the Wright Memorial Bridge and an hour back up the shore. Much of it is on regular asphalt roads, but the last ten miles is beach. Low tide only with half-deflated tires. No stores. No cops. Just a lot of sprawling houses, many of them built and used for destination weddings and the like.

We tried to do the trip right. We stopped at a crab shack and one of those trashy beach stores that has everything you want to look at but nothing you'd ever buy — cedar boxes with the outline of the outer banks burned into them, sea horses under epoxy, sand dollar earrings, wind chimes made from oyster knives. We loaded up at the Harris Teeter on the north end of Corolla, and then hit the beach an hour after dead low tide and went zipping among the odd herd of Spanish mustangs that run loose on that end of OBX and go wherever they please.

We got stuck once but backed out of it, and a misty gloom was settling in when some big, honking houses finally heaved into view. Ours was on the near end. Verre de Mer was a bit farther north. The 'community' had regular street signs, but the roads were all deep sand, so we wallowed to the house Gus had rented and hauled Ev inside first off.

Our place had a pool table next to the kitchen, three hot tubs on three different decks, an authentic Swedish sauna, two ovens and a warming drawer, and a TV attached to the ceiling, so if you wearied of stir frying, you just needed to look up. We left the Peltier place for the next day and ate grocery store fried chicken, played nine ball and tried to keep Ev out the Dickel. Him and Dwight spent interludes out on the back deck "just looking at the stars and stuff"(they told us), which seemed somehow to make them stoned.

Near midnight, Ev tried to deliver a speech, which proved part tragic biography, part Cindy longing, party grudging appreciation for the brotherhood of the crew, but then the bourbon and the pot overwhelmed him and, in mid testimonial, he fell asleep.

I wheeled him into a downstairs bedroom and spilled him onto a massive Cali king. Dwight went out to see the stars another time or two and then collapsed himself. Me and Gus probably sat up talking until very nearly three because it felt like the end of something. We'd taken on a chore and worked through it. We'd check out Peltier's beach house sometime in the a.m., spend another day together, and then bust the whole business up.

I got up with the sun like I always do — it's just the way God made me — and went out for a walk on the sand road, meaning to veer up a ways onto the beach.

It's a weird spot, Carova, a getaway place where you're essentially packed into a suburb. A fine suburb, but just houses one after another with no asphalt or curbstones in sight. A lot of sand piled up everywhere, a few misguided, half-assed attempts at landscaping. This was surely a section of shore the ocean would scour clean in time.

The whole neighborhood was eerily empty. It was just me and drifted sand and tufts of sea oats along with one rangy pony. He raised his head and gave me a look but stayed right where he was.

I'd gone maybe a quarter mile up the street and was about to turn to the beach at a junction when I glanced west and saw a truck sitting in the middle of the road, mired up to the axles. It was a wagon really. An old ambulance that looked to have been painted thinly with a roller. The words 'Henrico County' were peeking through.

I think I probably said, "Uh oh," like you do, and I believe I thought about going back to our house and picking up my pistol. I had nine bullets in the clip, and that Ruger was ready and lubricated, but I was well aware that ever since Joyce Sparks, I'd become a miserable shot.

I felt like I knew instinctively what was going on. Leonard, who'd kept tabs on Dustin Peltier, guessed he'd rather snitch out a dead man, which would help keep him uncontradicted, so he'd sent Juan or Diego, maybe both, to visit old Dusty and help him disappear. The Atlantic Ocean is a congenial spot for that.

I also knew that withdrawing to our house would be the sensible thing to do since Dustin Peltier deserved whatever those Guatemalans gave him, but I kept on going anyway. I told myself I'd just ease up on the Peltier house and confirm what I suspected with a look.

Along the way, I stopped every now and then to reconsider and listen. Nothing but gulls and the gusty sea breeze, so no reason to no go on. I did decide to arm myself and so checked around for some kind of weapon. I finally found one crammed in a nautical decoration by a house. It was some kind of lance, a harpoon maybe, all rusty and jagged, tetanus on a stick. I worked it free and took it with me, kept on north until I saw a sprawling house ahead with a royal blue Jeep in the driveway and Verre de Mer engraved on a post.

The front door was standing open, and I hung back and listened but didn't hear a thing. So I closed a little. Waited some more. Nothing but gulls and surf and the wind. I eased up onto the front porch, hung by the door — still silence from inside — and like a fool, I went on in, doing that thing I'd advised myself all along I ought not do.

The interior was cavernous, sanctuary sized, and open just about everywhere it could be. There were a lot of what looked like bedrooms off an intricate pickle-wood mezzanine overhead, and enough sofas and TV screens downstairs to suggest some kind of cushy air terminal.

I kept a wall to my back as I eased deeper in. Still no human sound but me. There was a restaurant-worthy kitchen, dining for twelve, illuminated wine nook, embers glowing in the blue enameled Scandi wood stove in the main room, but the look of the place had been spoiled by a human who'd made a considerable mess.

Every flat surface in the kitchen had at least one dirty dish on it, and there were loose sheets of paper scattered about in the sitting area like somebody had opened a fresh packet for the printer and had just thrown it into the air. There were words written in green marker on most of the sheets. Different words, one per page, but all in the same jagged hand. Oxter. Impignorate. Xertz. Ratoon. Gabelle. Quire. I finally recognized one of them — brontide — because it had stumped me once in a book.

I noticed on the coffee table a bowl full of daisy stuff. Daisy rings. Daisy key fobs. Daisy charms and decals. Like that. When I stepped over for a closer look, I noticed the shoes as well.

Shoe-bottoms actually. Diego's. He was face-down behind a sofa, or between a sofa anyway and a sideboard against the wall. His blood had seeped into a plush throw rug, and as I inched around for a better look, I could see he was punctured all over, little short of perforated. There were jagged holes in him about everywhere there was room for a hole to be.

I felt for a pulse. He was dead but still warm. I noticed one of the back sliding doors was cracked open about four inches and so went over to see how things were on the deck.

Interesting, as it turned out. Sullen Juan was in the jacuzzi, or rather he was on top of the cover but had weighed it down enough to get wet. He was perforated too, but his head was split open as well. I didn't need to guess with what because he was sprawled next to an ax, one of those shiny Swedish numbers that only people like Peltiers buy.

I decided to stick with my rusty harpoon and so I took it with me back inside and went upstairs to check out all the rooms. There were twelve of them, as it turned out, counting bedrooms and bathrooms both, and there was plenty of evidence of a slob in residence who'd moved from west to east fouling everything on the way. It looked like he'd sleep until the sheets got nasty and then move onto the next. As best I could tell, he was out of beds, probably out of socks as well.

There was more scattered paper upstairs, more green writing. Dehisce. Abderian. Qualtagh. Thelemic. Estrapade. Possibly a homicidal Scrabble freak.

I paused in the last bedroom to look out onto the beach. The tide was in. There was a barge on the horizon wallowing south behind a tug.

I called Gus.

"Hey," she said.

"He's here."

"Right," she said. "I know."

It's hard to run in sand, the deep loose kind, but I made short work of the trip back, since fear's a powerful motivator, and I didn't want to get back just in time to find my people perforated. Our door was standing open too, and I charge straight on in, me and my rusty harpoon and my active fear of carnage, but there they all were by the pool table looking all right. Ev in his chair, Gus and Dwight on the love seat. Dustin Peltier was standing before him with a frog gig in his hand.

He was shirtless. Nearly pantless too. He had on cargo shorts that were hanging half off his hips. He was bony, sunken, pallid and blotchy. He looked unwell in just about every way a human can. He didn't even glance at me at first, was busy with something on the pool table. It turned out to be our file on him, dumped out and spread on the felt. His interest was in one thing alone, our photo of younger Dustin. It was the one with the sun-streaked hair and the pink, peeled nose.

It delighted him. He giggled. Leonard had told us he laughed a lot.

As he picked up the photo with his free hand, I noticed that his frog gig had chunks and scraps of

Guatemalan tissue on the barbs. He seemed to approve of his younger self. He laughed some more and then he spoke.

"Encomium," he said and tapped his wooden gig handle on floor three times.

He had the look in his eyes of a man who was either hopelessly over-medicated or in need of intervention and not medicated at all.

"Mr. Peltier," I said, which didn't earn me even a glance. He was still busy with the photograph and said once more, "Encomium."

That wasn't a word I had a handle on, so it was gibberish to me at the time. I suspect now he was offering up his own nut job congratulations on the fact that we'd figured out the who and the where and were getting a front row seat on the why. Encomium. It had what he needed for a word — a bit obscure, a little Latin formal, and he could let it mean both eulogy and praise.

He raised his frog gig, shook it. He laughed again. He screamed.

I'd dealt with my share of nuts before, particularly back in uniform when every precinct had unhinged regulars you did your best to appease and shift around. I had experience with mutterers mostly and one lady who wept and shrieked, but the only hopping mad guy I'd ever seen — off the planet entirely — had been cuffed in the back of cruiser where he was trying to chew the upholstery. He'd had a Dustin Peltier look in his eyes, a blend of animal terror and unhinged delight.

I took a step towards Peltier. To the extent I had a plan, I meant to put myself between him and my crew if I could. Then it would be him with his frog gig and me with my rusty harpoon, and I felt like I had a decent chance to take him.

But when I moved, he moved. He shifted anyway like a snake would, adjusting to meet me. When I took a second step, he brought the gory business end of his gig far closer to Ev than I cared for, so I showed him a palm and stopped right where I was.

"Encomium," he said again and gestured with the photo, raised it over his head and cackled.

I slipped a bit closer, to the back of the love seat, which put me right behind Gus and Dwight. Dwight was wearing Roy Rogers jammies with Roy and Dale and Trigger and Bullet, Buttermilk even too.

"Encomium," I said.

Dustin Peltier showed the photo of his blonde self explicitly to me. Offered it even. I took it and raised it over my head like he had and laughed. He grunted, which I took as a display of wigged-out approval. Then he decided he wanted it back right away and snatched it from me and screamed.

Gus caught my eye and directed my attention to an item on the side table next to her. My Ruger wrapped in its greasy golf towel, which was four feet away from me at that moment, so nearly within reach.

I'd gotten absurdly gun careful since I'd killed a bystander, which up until that moment had seemed entirely reasonable to me, but seeing that lumpy oily towel invited me to picture what pulling my gun out and using it would mean. First I'd have to unwrap it. Then I'd have to unwrap the clip as well, which I kept in a piece of moleskin apart and separate from the pistol. Fortunately, the clip was loaded but only with four rounds because I'd found if I stored it with ten or fifteen, the works were sure to stick. I'd need to slap the clip in and put a bullet in the breach, switch off the safety with my thumb, and if Dustin Peltier was still in the county and available for it, I could squeeze off a round and very likely plug him from where I was.

So, yes, my pistol was almost handy, but some assembly would be required. I spared a moment to revile Feliks with a 'k', exotic bird smuggler and thoroughgoing source of grief.

Dustin Peltier got fixed on Ev for some reason. The boy just had on his tidy whiteys, must have come straight from bed, and his useless legs looked shrunken and wasted while from his gut up he was hale and stout.

Peltier who stated at Ev and finally told him, "Qualtagh."

At least I'd known encomium was a word. Qualtagh?

Peltier turned towards our bank of east windows that looked out on the dunes and, through the creases, we could see the Atlantic surf. He made a war-like gesture with his frog gig and shouted, "Pandiculation!" twice.

Then he tapped his gig handle three times on the floor and laughed (Belia would have said) like a drain.

ii

I think we all went through our version of it
three or four times apiece, first to a trio of
uniformed Corolla cops and then to their sergeant
and then a detective.

"Drugs, you think?" the sergeant asked me.
He'd had a personal interaction with Dusty a few
weeks earlier when Dusty had shoved a woman at
the Kangaroo Mart.

"Don't know. Did say he had a brain problem.
Told us something fell out."

"Of his brain?"

I nodded. "Said he could hear it rattling." I
tapped myself on the sternum just the way Dusty
had done it.

The sergeant gave the matter some extended
thought and then declared, "I think it's drugs."

It was way too weird for drugs, far more like a
brain not working because something had fallen
out. That and maybe a touch of thesaurus
poisoning just from the way he kept on with
words. Nidorosity. Sphallolalia. Causeuse.
Hadeharia. Jentacular. Xerophagy. He'd say them

a few times and then move onto the next, say them usually to Ev who'd tell him back, "Yeah."

That's how it went for, I guess, twenty minutes, which felt like a day and a half. Peltier eventually arrived at the brain stuff, and it almost sounded sensible by then. Oh, that's your trouble. Some part you needed fell out. There was surely something bad wrong with him, and it might as well have been a gap in his nut.

"Y'all bring this thing?" the sergeant asked me. They'd bagged the tip of my harpoon by then.

I shook my head and pointed vaguely. "Picked it up outside."

I'd been planning, coming up with the steps I'd need to take to intervene. Dustin Peltier kept spewing his words and making the odd threatening frog gig move towards Ev. He'd laugh and swing his barbs Ev's way, bring them close and then pull them back, while I stood there deciding how exactly I'd unwrap my gun and shoot him. Like I've said, I don't improvise terribly well, so I was doing my usual constipated thing.

"Right here, you say?" the sergeant asked and touched his torso almost precisely where the rusty tip had gone in.

"Yeah," I said and nodded.

It was Gus, of course. Dustin Peltier finally poked Ev with his gig, broke the skin only a little, but that was enough for Gus. She reached back and took my harpoon. It was probably partly the mother in her and partly the crewmate and friend. No planning for Gus. No laying out steps and organizing procedure. There was a lance at hand, and she rammed it home, speared the guy just below the ribs.

There was nothing shy about that thrust, nothing half-hearted and exploratory. Gus shoved the rusty steel tip six inches in, through flesh and gizzard and anything else that happened to be in the way.

If anything, Dustin Peltier looked offended. Gus pulled the tip out, and we all watched him. He put a hand to his wound as the blood came, and then he laughed again.

I was unwrapping my Ruger by then, but by the time I had it set and loaded, Dustin Peltier was off the back deck and on his way into the dunes. He'd just turned and left the house. He had one hand on the hole Gus had made, and his precious frog gig was in the other.

"Went through there?" The sergeant pointed at the crease in the dunes that led to the beach.

I nodded.

"Running?"

I shook my head. He'd walked like a man who had a place to be but time enough to get there.

We watched him, all four us. We'd gone out on the deck to do it. Me with my pistol. Gus with the harpoon. All of them underdressed for the weather. A wild pony had a look and a sniff at Dustin Peltier as he passed, heading straight for the tide line. The man never slowed or wavered.

"He killed those Guatemalans," I told them all.

"How?" Dwight asked.

"Mostly with that."

He had the gig high overhead by then. He'd raised it and was gesturing with it as he walked into the water, pumping his arm in what looked like triumph on his way into the surf.

Nobody chimed in with commentary. Nobody needed an explanation. We were watching a crazy man do what crazy men get up to. He was waist deep and then chest deep, and then he made a little dive and was gone, like the lord of the sea heading back to the deep, where he'd come from.

We watched the surf and waited. The gig soon came cartwheeling onto the beach, but Dustin Peltier failed to roll in. The sea had taken him, at least for a while. We watched for him, but it was just gulls and foam. A couple of horses. Shiny black porpoises in the middle distance. I heard

Gus on the phone with the Corolla PD trying to make them understand.

Instinctively and without any prior connivance, we'd all decided not to tell those Corolla cops terribly much about our case. There was no ulterior motive to it. That's my feeling anyway. It was just too much of a lift for the sort of police who wrote tickets and jiggled doorknobs. Accounting for who'd done what and why exactly was probably more than they wanted to know.

So they talked to us all separately, the way you do, and we gave them the bare facts of what had happened. A nut job had roamed into our rental house and been nutty there for a while. We'd defended ourselves. He'd walked in the surf. Hell of a thing. Who could explain it? The cops didn't seem to care since they had three dead in Carova, which was excitement enough to hold them for a bit.

Once I got loose on the deck, I made a phone call. Benny answered straightaway. I could hear Handel and the tires on the asphalt.

"We found Dustin Peltier," I told him and then explained about Juan and Diego. "Looks like life's about to get easy for Leonard." He had three corpses to snitch on now and nobody to bite back. Well, almost nobody.

Benny told me what I'd hoped for. "Can't have that," he said.

One of the forensic guys backed into the Hummer since yacht-sized and yellow didn't make it somehow visible enough. That distracted Gus for a bit and left me time sit with the boys. We were out of the wind on the screen porch while the techs took their samples inside.

They wanted reasons, Dwight and Ev, and looked like they'd settle for whatever I had.

"You heard him," I told them. "Something fell out."

They grumbled and objected. That was less than satisfying.

"Is this what justice feels like?" Dwight asked.

I told him, "Yeah." Told him, "Pretty much."

We were a hell of a lot less jolly on the trip home, and both Colby and big Jeremy had gotten their notice and were waiting for us on my doorstep. They were just sitting there on the lip of the porch having what looked like a manly chat, probably a blend of Redskins and gas mileage.

Jeremy tried to be big about the Hummer damage, made noises about Gus' safe return being the only thing that that mattered, but he kept circling to the battered side and shaking his head and sighing.

"The body washed up," Colby told us. "Three or four miles south." I guess he was about as happy as he got. The man had done a lot of nothing but had still ended up with cases settled and lowlives scoured from the earth.

Big Jeremy tried to shake my hand out in the driveway as I was unloading bags.

"Remember that eye you gave her?" I said of and then punched him crisply twice. Vengeance, eventually and in time.

I was making a run for stroganoff fixings when I thought of Vilmer Demarest and felt like I had a duty to fill him in straightaway. So I detoured up and over to Magnolia Hills but couldn't find him anywhere. His stunted piece of hallway was empty, and there was a lady in his old room, a heavily scented woman with a French Provincial dresser and several photos of a terrier.

When I checked in at the desk, the girl there went off to nab an administer to properly give me the news.

She escorted me into the solarium and sat beside me on a sofa. She had on one of those blouses that tied at the neck into an oversized sateen bow. The lobes and tucks were all cockeyed, so the whole time she talked to me, I just wanted to reach over and undo the thing, tie it all over again.

Vilmer had quit life. That was the message, though that woman — her name was Kimberly — would only tell me that he'd "passed". She was keen for me to know he'd gone peacefully, that he'd "yielded in his sleep"(she called it). I'd missed him by a mere week and a half, and at first, I regretted he'd not heard what we'd discovered — that Abigail Tucker (very possibly his daughter) had died at the hands of over-privileged nutter scum whose business associates and hangers-on had dumped her in the forest. But the more I thought about it, even right there in the moment, the less it seemed the sort of thing that Vilmer should ever have heard. The longer I sat with Kimberly, the more my timing felt just right.

"I have something for you," she told me and pulled a photo out of her pocket.

It was snapshot they'd laminated, an institutionalized bit of thoughtfulness, an informal picture of Vilmer Demarest sitting outside on a bench. It didn't look terribly recent because his eyes were too clear and his nose hair too short. I figured they'd taken it when he arrived at the place, a thing they did for everybody so they could hand you a keepsake when the passing had happened and the glorious end had come.

I was reminded of a veterinary surgeon I'd taken my mutt to once. He had a girl on staff who did nothing but write I'm-sorry-your-dog-died cards.

I thanked Kimberly and swung by the grocery store, bought egg noodles and ground beef along with a decent bottle of zinfandel, and we spilled out some for Vilmer Demarest — possible father of Abigail Tucker, Sunoco man for certain, horn dog extraordinaire.

~~~

We put Vilmer Demarest's original file back together so we could return it to his niece's car shed and tell her how things had ended up.

We all rode out to Chuckatuck one afternoon and met up Shirley Mathis' in her driveway where Ev and Dwight did most of the talking and explained in polite detail how case 873946/B had turned out.

Vilmer Demarest was buried in a family plot on the crown of a slope behind Shirley Mathis' house. We had to drag Ev backwards through a pasture to get him up there. They were still waiting on the headstone carver. The grave itself was raw clay. There were various Demarests scattered about, and Vilmer had been laid in next to his wife whose name was waiting for his on the marble marker above a Bible verse. "We would rather be away from the body and at home with the Lord."

I drove by the swampside house one day, and a man was cleaning the front yard with a loader. He let me stand and watch him for a while before he throttled down.

"Want a dog?" He pointed. He had the nasty mongrel in a kennel in the back of his truck.

I shook my head. "Leonard still here?"

"Think it's empty."

"You mind?"

He shrugged and throttled back up, so I went into the house. The front door frame was still splintered, and somebody had hauled all the furniture out, had left behind just grit and mildew, a few nasty rugs and some scarred flooring, along with a half dozen paperback books stacked on a window sill. Leon Uris. Dr. Wayne Dyer. Willa Cather. Thomas Carlyle.

I decided Leonard had bugged out since he was just the sort of vermin who was sure to be lucky that way. I'd certainly not heard any different, and then Benny called me up to drive him. Marco was getting the snip because his wife was tired of babies, which meant two days behind the wheel for me. I showed up and untarped the Chrysler, gave it a light buff with the chamois, and had the temperature where Benny liked it by the time he and Mags came out of the house.

She looked good, unmarked and smiling. I got my Handel instructions from Benny. He had new Ariodante. Sofi von Otter with Minkowski conducting. I put the disc in and turned it up.

"One stop," he said and sent me in the general direction of Barrel Point.

The opera was into the second act by the time we'd reached a stretch of piney woods where Benny told me, "Hold on," so he and Mags could reconnoiter.

They found the road they wanted just down from a run of high-tension power lines, and I turned where they told me and headed down a gravel track with scrubby thickets and slash pines on either side, Franzia boxes in the ditches.

Mags found the gap in the scrub they were after, and she was the one who told me, "Whoa."

I stopped in the road. We all got out, and I followed them into the woods. It took them a little wandering to find the spot that they were after, but once they'd noticed a stump they both could agree on, it was a straight line in from there.

We reached a nasty, little clearing where the saplings were mostly dead, and the ground was covered in bark and needles except for a spot that had been turned over. Mags went straight to it and spat ferociously onto the ground. Then she left me and Benny alone in the woods, headed straight back to the car.

Benny raised his quoting finger and told me, "Justice cannot sleep forever." He jabbed the loose earth with his dogwood staff. "But maybe Leonard can."

Then Benny followed Mags and left me alone in the clearing, and I sure didn't need any help with the symmetry of the thing. A dead girl in the woods at Simmons Gap, dead Leonard wherever this was, and a lot of years and misery in between.

I felt like I ought to say something, even if only for me and Leonard, so I cast around for a fitting remark to air but just came up with, "Encomium."

Back at the house, the gang had been cleaning. They'd boxed up our command center stuff and had given the rest of the place a scour. Dwight and Gus had anyway. Ev, I was told when I stepped inside, was enjoying some private time with pep squad Cindy in my command center/ spare bedroom.

I didn't tell them about Leonard. I'd decided to keep that for me and Gus in the small hours.

"Did Cindy need revirginating?" I asked.

"Define 'need'," Gus instructed me.

And that's about when Ev started shouting. "I hear you, Bob Raymond. Come here."

The spare bedroom door was shut, and I wasn't eager to go in.

"Bob!"

But Ev wasn't going to drop it, so I knocked and got a, "Come."

I opened the door on Ev and Cindy doing nothing much at all. There was a lone page on our corkboard, a photograph spat out of the printer.

Cindy was sitting cross-legged on the desk and holding Ev by the fingers

Ev grinned and snorted. He pointed at the corkboard, so I stepped over to have a look.

He'd made a copy of a newspaper story, which was half photograph, half type. The date at the top was November 2004. Body of Emporia Man Found In Tree. The photograph was of the tree alone, a towering tulip poplar.

I scanned some of the copy. The usual stuff. A lot of palaver to say nobody had any idea how he got there or what he was doing with antifreeze in his lungs. A stone cold whodunnit going on thirteen years. Why not, I asked myself, start again instead of quit?

But I can play dumb with the best of them, so I went slack and pointed, asked Ev and Dwight and Gus and even Cindy too, "What's this?"

58901643R00172

Made in the USA
Middletown, DE
08 August 2019